Bondi Beach Medics

Beachside rescues and sun-kissed romance!

With most of their childhoods spent roaming
Australia's shorelines with their nomadic parents,
Sydney was the only place that the Carlson siblings
made their home.

And now they're back! Living under the same roof
and practicing the medicine they love. Saving lives
in its hospitals and on its beaches. After all,
they never could resist the call of the surf!

Yet as the familiar embrace of Bondi Beach's
coastline welcomes them in life and career,
it's the call of love that could truly make
this place their home.

Discover Poppy's story in
Rescuing the Paramedic's Heart
Available now!

And look out for Jet, Daisy and Lily's stories
Coming soon!

D0059738

Dear Reader,

Thank you for picking up this book, which is the first in my four-book Bondi Beach Medics series.

I'd like to introduce you to Poppy Carlson, the third of four siblings—Lily, Jet, Poppy and Daisy. They are an ED doctor, a lifeguard, a paramedic and a pediatric nurse, each with their own tale to tell.

I loved the idea of exploring their lives across a series and I'm excited to see where they go. I hope you enjoy Poppy and Ryder's love story and come with me when I move ahead to Jet, Daisy and Lily!

I promise drama, adversity, love and laughter set against a backdrop of sun, surf and summer at Australia's busiest and most famous beach.

I'd love to hear from you if you've enjoyed this story or any of my others. You can visit my website, emily-forbesauthor.com, or drop me a line at emilyforbes@internode.on.net.

Emily

RESCUING THE PARAMEDIC'S HEART

EMILY FORBES

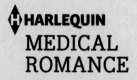

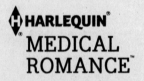

HARLEQUIN®
MEDICAL
ROMANCE™

PLEASE RECYCLE
THIS PRODUCT IS RECYCLABLE

Recycling programs
for this product may
not exist in your area.

ISBN-13: 978-1-335-40437-4

Rescuing the Paramedic's Heart

Copyright © 2021 by Emily Forbes

This edition published by arrangement with Harlequin Books S.A.

For questions and comments about the quality of this book, please contact us at CustomerService@Harlequin.com.

Harlequin Enterprises ULC
22 Adelaide St. West, 40th Floor
Toronto, Ontario M5H 4E3, Canada
www.Harlequin.com

Printed in U.S.A.

Emily Forbes is an award-winning author of medical romance for Harlequin. She has written over twenty-five books and has twice been a finalist for the Australian Romantic Book of the Year Award, which she won in 2013 for her novel *Sydney Harbor Hospital: Bella's Wishlist*. You can get in touch with Emily at emilyforbes@internode.on.net, or visit her website at emily-forbesauthor.com.

Books by Emily Forbes

Harlequin Medical Romance

London Hospital Midwives
Reunited by Their Secret Daughter

Nurses in the City
Reunited with Her Brooding Surgeon

The Christmas Swap
Waking Up to Dr. Gorgeous

Tempted & Tamed
A Doctor by Day...
Tamed by the Renegade
A Mother to Make a Family

One Night That Changed Her Life
Falling for His Best Friend
Rescued by the Single Dad
Taming Her Hollywood Playboy
The Army Doc's Secret Princess

Visit the Author Profile page
at Harlequin.com for more titles.

For James,

Twenty-four years as husband and wife
and I'm having as much fun now as I did
when we were first married!

I couldn't do this without you.

With love, now and always,

Emily

16 March 2021

**Praise for
Emily Forbes**

"Ms. Forbes has delivered a delightful read in
this book where emotions run high because of
everything this couple go through on their journey
to happy ever after…and where the chemistry
between this couple was strong; the romance was
delightful and had me loving these two together."
—*Harlequin Junkie* on *Rescued by the Single Dad*

CHAPTER ONE

'EASY? KEEP AN eye on Backpackers' Express, I reckon we might have trouble.'

Jet Carlson's voice came through the radio, catching Ryder's attention as he stood beside the lifeguard buggy. Jet was up in the circular lifeguard tower that overlooked Bondi Beach, keeping watch over the one-kilometre curve of white sand, issuing updates to the lifeguards on patrol. Ryder reached into the buggy and picked up his binoculars and scanned the beach, looking towards the troublesome rip to the south. He picked out a dark-haired man swimming alone where the first waves were breaking as the Pacific Ocean rolled into the shore.

He picked up the walkie-talkie, certain he was looking at the same man Jet had spotted. 'Copy that, Central, I see him,' he responded.

He stood by the buggy as he kept his eyes on the swimmer. The water to the man's left was deceptively calm between two sets of rolling waves. Ryder knew the tide was turning and the calm water indicated a passage of water flowing out to sea. If the man got any closer, he'd be pulled out to sea with the tide.

It was the danger period, after lunch on a hot Sunday. It wasn't peak season yet; it was only the middle of spring and school hadn't finished for the year but the beach was still busy. Holidaymakers, shift workers and backpackers all flocked to Bondi at any time of the year. The tide was going out and the notorious rip was going to cause grief. Most likely to an unsuspecting tourist.

No matter how hard the lifeguards tried, it was impossible to get all the beachgoers to swim between the flags. Ryder knew it was sometimes because they didn't understand English or the dangers or where to swim, at other times they just chose to ignore the lifeguards and the risks, thinking their swimming ability was better than it was or that the warnings were some kind of joke or scaremongering tactics and the treacherous conditions wouldn't affect them. It didn't help matters that the main access point to the beach was closest to the dangerous southern end.

But no matter what the reason was for

swimmers ending up in the wrong place, the lifeguards' job was to look after them all. The drunk, the stubborn, the unlucky.

Life was precious and Ryder felt a strong sense of responsibility and, at the end of the day, a strong sense of satisfaction in a job well done, whether that had been saving a life or just preventing a disaster. Not every day brought an emergency, although there was always some excitement, but a quiet day on the beach was preferable to one filled with drama.

Either way he enjoyed the work. It was interesting and varied and he met people from all over the world and from all walks of life and he reckoned that would hold him in good stead for his future career as a psychologist. If he could cope with the Bondi beachgoers, he could cope with anything.

He hadn't worked at Bondi long. It had only been a couple of months since he'd been offered a position and had become one of several lifeguards employed by the local council to patrol the popular beach three hundred and sixty-five days of the year. It was a highly coveted job and usually went to qualified Sydneysiders who had grown up surfing the waves at the local beaches and had years of experience of the conditions.

He'd had years of experience as a surfer and as a lifeguard at Cottesloe Beach in Western Australia but that was on the opposite side of the country, on the shores of the Indian Ocean. But the Pacific Ocean was familiar to him—he'd spent his childhood surfing the breaks at Byron Bay, on the coast north of Bondi. The ocean on Australia's east coast had been home to him until one fateful day, just before his eighteenth birthday, when he'd been uprooted from everything that was special to him and moved thousands of kilometres away to the other side of the continent.

Eventually he'd settled in his new home and when he'd arrived in Bondi, part way through his transcontinental road trip, he hadn't planned on staying but he'd been offered a temporary position and it had been too good to refuse.

He'd landed in Bondi at just the right time. Two lifeguards had sustained serious injuries that would keep them off the beach for several months over the busy summer period and the council had been desperate to employ qualified replacements. Ryder had fitted the bill and, fortunately for him, he also had a personal reference from his childhood friend, Jet Carlson, the lifeguard who was currently manning the tower and giving Ryder his instructions.

He was happy with temporary. He knew he couldn't stay for ever as he was needed back west, but for the moment this was good. Casual work would allow him to extend his break and make sure he was refreshed and energised when he went home.

It was a perfect situation, he thought as he had a quick glance along the beach, trying to figure out if there was anyone else keeping an eye on the man he had under watch. Was anyone else aware of his position? In situations like this it could be helpful to speak to someone who knew the swimmer. It could help determine how competent they were in the water.

But he didn't really need confirmation, he'd bet his next pay cheque on the fact that this guy wasn't a strong swimmer. He could see him pushing off the bottom, not wanting to get out of his depth, but the outgoing tide was already taking him further from the beach and the minute he got washed off the sandbar he'd be in deep water.

As Ryder watched, a wave broke over the man's head, submerging him. That second or two when he went under was long enough to make him lose his footing. As he surfaced, he was swept into the channel and away from the beach.

He was in trouble.

'Easy?' Jet's voice came through the radio, using Ryder's nickname.

'I'm on it.' Ryder leapt out of the buggy, whipped off his distinctive blue lifeguard shirt, grabbed the rescue board from the rack on the side of the all-terrain vehicle and sprinted into the surf. He threw his board in front of him and dived onto it. He paddled strongly out past the small waves that were crashing onto the shore, past the swimmers who were oblivious to the drama unfolding a few metres off the beach, past the break.

He scanned the sea as pulled his board through the water and caught a brief glimpse of the man's head as it appeared behind a wave before he lost sight of him again. He dug deep, paddling harder, knowing time was of the essence. His shoulder muscles bunched and already he could feel the burn but he was used to that. He was breathing deeply, his lungs straining, and he could feel his heart racing but he wouldn't stop. He was getting close now.

He crested a small wave just in time to see the man go under again.

Two more strokes.

He reached over the side of the board, plunging his arm into the water up to his elbow. He scooped his arm through the water but came up empty. He could see the man's dark hair. He leaned over further, plunging his whole arm into the ocean, the sea reaching to his armpit, and this time his fingers grabbed hold of the man's head. He pulled him to the surface by a fistful of hair. He knew it would hurt but having your hair pulled was a small price to pay in exchange for your life.

He dragged the man from the water, holding him by one arm. He wasn't breathing. Ryder needed to get him securely onto the rescue board and back to shore. The man was of slight build and probably weighed no more than seventy kilograms. Ryder was six feet three inches tall, fit and strong, a muscular ninety kilograms with no excess weight, but even so he strained with the effort of pulling a dead weight out of the water.

He grabbed his patient under his armpits and hauled him up, draping him across the board. He pulled his legs out of the ocean and waited to see if he would start breathing on his own.

The man coughed twice, expelling sea

water, and began breathing. Now Ryder just had to get him back to the beach.

He got the man balanced, getting him to lie on his stomach in front of him. It was a long paddle back to shore and he didn't want the board tipping. He didn't want to lose his patient and have to go through the process of getting him out of the water a second time.

As Ryder brought his board onto the beach two dark-haired women hurried down to the water's edge. His patient fell off the board into the shallow water as the rescue board hit the sand. Ryder grabbed his board with one hand and hooked his other hand under the man's armpit, helping him to his feet. His legs were shaky, the small waves almost knocking him off balance, and Ryder kept hold of him, helping to keep him upright.

'Thank you. Thank you.' The man had recovered enough to speak but his English was heavily accented.

'No worries,' Ryder replied, even though it *was* a worry. Beachgoers needed to be aware of the dangers. He didn't want to be rescuing the same man again today, something that had happened many times before.

'Do you see those flags?' he said as he pointed north along the beach. 'Red and yellow? You must swim between the flags.' He gave the warning, even though he doubted he would be understood, but he had a duty to explain the risks and to attempt to get them to follow the rules.

'Yes, yes.' The man and his friends all nodded but Ryder suspected none of them fully comprehended his caution.

'Here—very dangerous,' he emphasised as he waved his hand out to sea in the direction of the rip and tried one last time to stress the need to avoid this area, but he didn't have time to repeat himself, or to give any other advice, before he heard Jet's voice again from the radio in the buggy.

'Easy? There's another one in Backpackers'. I'm sending the jet-ski out but you'll be faster.'

Backpackers' Rip hadn't finished creating chaos yet and the day was going downhill fast.

'No worries,' he replied. 'I've got it.'

The Asian tourists were still thanking him as he picked up his board, turned and sprinted back into the water.

'Hello! I'm here. Anyone home?'

Lily jumped as she heard the front door slam and her sister's voice calling for her.

Poppy had arrived and the energy in the house kicked up a notch, swirling around Lily as the serenity of the day evaporated. From the time she could walk Poppy's life had moved at a million miles an hour. She was loud and fast and hectic. By comparison, Lily and Daisy, the eldest and youngest Carlson sisters, were quiet. Only their brother, Jet, could give Poppy a run for her money in the volume stakes and that was only at certain times. Jet had two settings—quietly monosyllabic or loud and boisterous. Poppy constantly operated at full volume and top speed, as if there were too many things to get done, no time to stop.

Poppy was standing just inside the front hall. She had two bags slung over her shoulders but she dumped them on the floor to hug her sister.

Lily hugged her tightly before stepping back to look at her younger sibling.

Poppy was a mixture of her older and younger sisters physically but there wasn't much of either of them in Poppy's personality. Lily wondered momentarily how disruptive Poppy's arrival was going to be. But when Poppy had called and said she needed a place to stay, Lily hadn't hesitated. They might be like chalk and cheese in many ways but they were family and, as the eldest of the Carlson tribe, Lily had always made her siblings her priority. Poppy could be exhausting but Lily would deal with the logistics of her arrival just like she dealt with everything else— almost everything else, she amended silently, knowing there was one issue she was continuing to ignore. Having Poppy stay might turn out to be a bonus—someone else's drama might be a good distraction from the mess of her own personal life.

'Why don't you put your things in here?' Lily pointed to the bedroom off the hall on their right. 'And I'll put the kettle on.'

Poppy threw her bags onto the bed. This room was at the front of the house that Lily used to share with her husband. Poppy wondered if Lily had spoken to Otto recently or if she was still struggling with what had happened between them. She'd had a difficult time and she had Poppy's sympathy.

Thinking about Lily's love life reminded her to try calling Craig. Again. She took her phone out of her bag and brought up his number but, for the second time in as many hours, her call went to voice mail. This time she left a message, letting him know she'd arrived safely and asking him to call her back.

She ended the call, annoyed that he hadn't phoned her after the last message. He would have checked his phone. Surely, he'd want to know she'd reached Sydney safely?

She sighed, knowing there was nothing she could do about it. She kicked off her shoes and headed for the kitchen.

Lily's house was tall and narrow, it spanned four levels but was only one room wide, and it was in a magnificent position, perched on the hill at the southern end of Bondi with an incredible view looking east over the ocean and north over the famous beach. The kitchen opened onto a deck and Poppy stepped out and tipped her face to the sky, letting the sun warm her skin. She inhaled and let the scent of the sea wash over her. She'd missed the beach.

She had spent most of the past nine years living in Brisbane, which, despite it being the capital of Queensland, was severely lacking in beaches. Having grown up in Byron Bay on the New South Wales north coast, the ocean was in her blood and it was good to be able to step outside and see the waves and smell the salt air.

'Where's Daisy?' Poppy asked as Lily handed her a mug of tea and sat beside her on a high stool that afforded them a view over the sea. The kitchen was on the entrance level but the ground sloped away below the deck and Poppy could look down into the garden or out over the ocean.

'She's at work, she's on an early and I have to go in shortly as there are a couple of patients I need to check.' Both Lily and Daisy worked at Bondi General Hospital. Lily was a first-year resident and Daisy was a paediatric nurse. 'I thought we could have a family dinner tonight, though, I've asked Jet, too. He's on duty today but finishes at seven.'

Their brother, Jet, who was sandwiched between Lily and Poppy in the family order, worked as a lifeguard, employed by the local council to patrol Bondi Beach and neighbouring Tamarama and Bronte beaches. It was a full-time job and one that Poppy knew he loved. Jet's personality was perfectly suited to the role—every day was different, the job kept him fit, he was surrounded by blokes but had plenty of female attention. Some of the aspects appealed to Poppy—namely the excitement and variety—but it wasn't a career she wanted. The financial reward wasn't generous enough for her and job security was another factor. Jet had to prove his physical fitness every year—that wasn't a problem for him, he was a professional athlete as well and trained hard, but while Poppy maintained her fitness for her career as a paramedic she felt that having to pass a test every year to keep her job would be stressful.

'So, how was the drive?'

'Fine.' Poppy had split the long drive south from Queensland to New South Wales over two days to make it manageable. 'I didn't have any dramas but it was a little lonely. It would have been nice to share it with Craig.' Craig's employer was transferring him to Sydney and Poppy had applied to join the New South Wales Ambulance service in order to move with him. But Craig was currently busy on a large project that had delayed his move and Poppy had found herself relocating to Sydney ahead of him.

'Has he booked a flight to come down for a weekend?' Lily asked.

Poppy shook her head. 'Not yet. He said he'll come down in a fortnight's time. I'm hoping that will give me time to line up a few rentals to look at when he's here.'

'What does his time frame look like now? Is he still thinking his move will be a few months away?'

Poppy nodded. 'He doesn't think he'll get here for another three months. He reckons he'll need to work through Christmas and won't be able to move until the end of January. One or the other of us will travel up or down every two or three weeks.' Poppy shrugged and added, 'Lots of couples have long-distance relationships, it'll be fine.' It wasn't until she saw Lily's stricken expression that she realised what she'd said. 'Sorry, Lil, I wasn't thinking.'

Poppy waited for Lily's response to her apology but Lily was silent, her face blank. Lily and her husband had been living separately for almost two years. Otto was in London, doing his medical speciality training, and Lily should have been there with him, but their plans had gone awry and Lily had come home.

'How is Otto?' Poppy asked, filling the silence.

'Can we not talk about this now?' Lily said as she stood and picked up their empty mugs. Poppy knew she was using the activity as a means of avoiding eye contact. 'I need to get to work.'

'Of course.' Poppy didn't want to upset her further. She'd hoped Lily and Otto would have made some progress in healing their relationship or, if that wasn't possible, at least made some progress in deciding how they were going to move forward. She knew their separation was about more than just physical distance but she also suspected the distance was making things more difficult. She hoped they would eventually be able to resolve their differences and while she wasn't about to insist that Lily talk to her right now she did make a mental note to broach the topic again. She needed to check on Lily's well-being.

Poppy changed into her bikini, shorts and a T-shirt as Lily left for work. She'd go to the beach for a quick swim, she decided, say hi to her brother and then come back and make a start on dinner.

She checked her phone for what felt like the hundredth time as she slid her feet into her flip-flops. Still nothing. She tossed it back on the bed. She wouldn't take it to the beach as she wasn't planning to be gone for long. If Craig called while she was out, she'd call him back later.

She left her car parked on the road in front of the house and walked down Edward Street towards the beach. After consecutive six-hour days in the car, driving from Brisbane to Sydney, she needed to stretch her legs and the fifteen-minute walk to Campbell Parade would help to clear the cobwebs.

She turned onto the pedestrian path and

walked along the promenade past the skate park and the mural wall towards the lifeguard tower.

She stopped before she reached the tower and leaned on the railing and looked out over the beach. The sun was behind her and the sea shone in the afternoon light. The sand was crisp and white and, despite the fact that it was not yet the summer holidays, the beach was busy. She took a deep breath, filling her lungs with the sea air, and stood for a moment, enjoying the feeling of warm sun on her skin as she watched the water.

The waves were small but she could spot the rips, the deceptively smooth water between breaking waves. She had years of experience as a surfer—growing up in Byron Bay, she and her siblings had learned to surf almost before they could walk—but she could see why the tourists and the locals who weren't familiar with the ocean could be fooled into thinking the rips were safe spots to swim.

She turned to the south to see if she could pick out Lily's house perched on the cliff before she spun on her heel and headed for the circular lifeguard tower. She knocked on the blue door and waited, if Jet wasn't in there someone would be able to tell her where he was.

'Poppy! You're here.' Jet grinned as he swung the door open. His welcoming smile was wide, his perfect teeth white and even in his tanned face. His blond hair was pulled back into a messy man bun but that was all Poppy had time to absorb before he stepped out of the tower and wrapped her in a tight hug. He stood well over six feet tall, and even with his slim but muscular athlete's build he managed to make her feel small. She was five feet seven inches, not short for a girl, but Jet made her feel petite.

He released her and dragged her into the tower where he introduced her to the other lifeguards.

'Guys, this is my little sister, Poppy. Poppy, meet the guys—Gibbo, Bluey and Dutchy.'

Poppy smiled at Jet's use of the guys' nicknames.

'Are you going to hang around here for a while?' he asked as Poppy finished saying hello.

'No, I just wanted to say hi. I'm going to have a swim and then head home. I hear you're coming for dinner.'

Jet nodded and looked as if he was about to say something else when the radio on the desk crackled into life.

'Central, this is Easy. We've got a problem down here, south of the flags.'

He held up one hand in Poppy's direction, asking her to wait as he grabbed the radio. 'Go ahead, Ryder.'

'The tourist I pulled from Backpackers', he's not looking great. I'm bringing him back to the tower for an assessment.'

Poppy's ears pricked up as she listened to the exchange. Ryder was an unusual name. She'd only ever known one and he had been Jet's best friend when they were at high school. He'd also been her first crush. But the Ryder she'd known had moved away when he was seventeen, breaking her young, impressionable heart in the process—although she'd kept that to herself—and she hadn't seen him since.

It couldn't be him, though, could it? Surely Jet would have said something.

'Ryder?' she said as Jet put the radio down.

'Yeah, Ryder Evans, you remember him?'

Of course she remembered him.

She could feel herself colouring as she thought about the last time she'd seen him. She hoped Jet didn't notice the blush she could feel creeping up her neck.

She nodded. 'You never told me he was in Sydney.'

'Didn't I?' Jet shrugged. 'Probably figured you wouldn't care, you haven't seen him for the best part of twelve years,' he said over his shoulder as he went to open the door to the tower.

He had a point. He wouldn't think it was important. It *wasn't* important really, although that didn't stop a frisson of nervousness from shooting through her at the thought of seeing him again. She hadn't thought about him for years, had finally let the idea of him go, yet at the mere mention of his name all the old feelings rose to the surface along with all the memories of how much he'd meant to her teenage self. She could instantly recall all her teenage fantasies and the memories made her blush.

The lifeguard buggy pulled to a stop at the bottom of the metal stairs that led from the sand to the tower entrance and Poppy's jaw dropped as a lifeguard jumped out. Tall and muscular, tanned and fit.

Was that Ryder?

She managed to close her mouth as she watched him help his patient out of the buggy and up the stairs.

She hung back, out of the way, as Ryder got the man into the tower and onto the treatment plinth. Jet went to assist, instructing Bluey to keep an eye on the beach. Poppy stayed near the desk by the windows. The lifeguards had a job to do and she didn't want to be a nuisance but staying out of the way also gave her a chance to check Ryder out unobserved. She knew he hadn't noticed her, he was too focussed on his patient.

The last time she'd seen him there had been a hint of the man he would become, of the man waiting to emerge, but he'd still been a gangly teenager. He'd been tall but he'd yet to have a fast growth spurt or develop the muscle definition that would come with adulthood. But all traces of adolescence had disappeared now. Now there was no hiding the man. And no ignoring the feeling of warmth that was spreading through her belly and into her groin. Poppy leaned on the desk, taking the weight off her suddenly shaky legs.

Fortunately Ryder had his back to her and wouldn't be aware of her reaction but she was very aware of him.

He'd grown even taller and he'd definitely filled out. He'd developed muscles where he hadn't had them before. He wore only a pair of black boardshorts with 'Lifeguard' emblazoned across his hips and she had plenty of opportunity to admire the view of sculpted muscles and smooth, tanned skin. His shoulders were broad, his biceps bulging, his waist narrow. He looked fit. He looked healthy. He looked magnificent.

She ran her gaze up the length of his spine and up his neck. She could see where the knobs of his vertebrae disappeared into his hair. He'd always had amazing hair, dark blond and thick, and at almost twenty-nine years of age it seemed he'd lost none of it.

Her gaze traced the line of his jaw. It was strong and square. He looked good, even better than she remembered, and she felt another rush of blood to her cheeks as her heart skittered in her chest.

Her hands gripped the edge of the desk as she observed him, keeping her fixed in place, and she wondered at the involuntary response. Was she stopping herself from crossing the room? While her rational mind might tell her that Ryder's unexpected appearance was of no consequence, it seemed her body had other ideas. Her palms were clammy and her mouth was dry and she suddenly felt like the sixteen-year-old schoolgirl she'd been when she'd last seen him.

When she had kissed him.

And he had kissed her back.

She knew from talking to her girlfriends that first kisses often weren't anywhere near as fabulous as they'd dreamed about but the kiss she and Ryder had shared had been everything she'd hoped for and more. It had been the biggest moment of her young life. It had *changed* her life.

She'd fallen in love.

First love.

She had only been a teenager but that hadn't made it any less real, any less all-encompassing, any less all-consuming.

And it hadn't made it any less painful when he'd walked out of her life.

CHAPTER TWO

Poppy knew it hadn't been Ryder's choice to leave but she'd spent many days—many months—waiting for him to acknowledge that he missed her as much as she missed him, but she'd heard nothing and the complete lack of contact had left her feeling foolish and embarrassed.

Their kiss had been everything she'd dreamt of but it obviously hadn't had the same impact on him. He'd probably forgotten all about it within days. But it had taken her much, much longer and now all those long-forgotten feelings came flooding back.

The anticipation, the joy and the delight. The spark, the excitement and the satisfaction. The pounding of her heart and the wobbling of her knees. Her nervousness and then her embarrassment over her teenage self and how she'd thrown herself at him. Unfortunately, her embarrassment had become her most powerful memory of the whole experience.

She hadn't been rejected as such but it had become fairly clear that she hadn't had the same lasting effect on him as he'd had on her.

She assumed he'd forgotten all about it. She could only hope so now. More than likely it was only seared into her memory. At least, if that was the case, maybe she'd get over her discomfiture. It would be difficult otherwise—especially as there was no denying he was now super-hot.

She stood in the corner of the tower, clutching the desk as if her life depended on it, and listened to the lifeguards' assessment of the patient as she brought her thoughts back to the present day.

The patient's English was far from fluent but even so it was obvious he was complaining of a headache and stomach pain. He was coughing intermittently. Poppy watched as Ryder slipped an oxygen mask over the man's nose and mouth and then took his blood pressure.

'BP one-forty over ninety. Pulse one hundred. I reckon we should keep him in the tower for observation,' Dutchy commented.

'Can you open your eyes for me, Tong?' Ryder asked. 'I think we should call the ambos just to be sure. He's drowsy and complaining of a headache. There's a good chance he's inhaled sea water and I reckon he's dehydrated and had a bit too much sun.' Ryder voiced his concerns about Tong's rapidly deteriorating condition.

'What do you think, Poppy?' Jet turned to Poppy.

Ryder turned too. 'Hey, Poppy, I didn't see you there.'

He smiled at her and she was grateful for the support of the desk. His smile was enough to fan the flames that were already racing through her and if it hadn't been for the furniture she suspected she'd be a messy puddle of oestrogen on the floor of the tower.

'Hello, Ryder.'

She did her best to hold his gaze even as she wondered why he was still able to affect her this way. This reaction was exactly why she steered clear of choosing boyfriends based on chemistry. She hated feeling out of control. Hated this feeling of losing control over her senses, her responses and her behaviour. Ever since she'd lost her heart to Ryder all those years ago she'd vowed not to let her emotions or her hormones carry her away again but, apparently, all it took was one smile from him and she felt like she was falling all over again.

Standing in the tower, clinging to the desk, an image of fairy-tale princesses trapped in castles, waiting for knights to rescue them, sprang to her mind before she told herself she was being ridiculous. She didn't need rescuing. She was perfectly content with her life. With Craig.

Yes, Craig. Remember Craig, she told herself. Safe, predictable Craig. He wouldn't distract her from her goals. He wouldn't let her down. He hadn't returned her calls yet but she knew he would. He was dependable. There were no great highs and lows. He was calm, and that was what she wanted. She knew where she was with Craig. She could remain focussed, protect her heart and keep control of her world. Her life was just how she liked it—simple, uncomplicated, safe.

She realised Jet was waiting with an expectant expression for her answer and she tried to remember what the question had been. 'Can you give me the history?' she asked.

'I pulled him out of Backpackers' Rip.' Poppy's question had been directed at Jet but the patient was Ryder's and he answered. 'He was completely submerged, not breathing initially, but he recovered spontaneously. He seemed to be okay and I left him with his friends but they came back to me and said he was complaining of a headache, dizziness and stomach pains. He's vomited a few times too. All typical symptoms of having inhaled water.'

His gaze was intense. She remembered that about him. How he used to watch and listen and make her feel like what she said was important.

'How long ago did you get him out of the water?'

'About an hour ago.'

Poppy knew there was always a risk of secondary drowning if someone was suspected to have inhaled water. Even if the risk was slight, it couldn't be ignored. 'I think he should at least be rehydrated and it's important that he understands the potential dangers of getting water in his lungs. He should probably have an X-ray of his lungs and he should definitely be monitored. Leave the oxygen on and call the ambulance—they can put him on a drip, take him to hospital and keep an eye on him. Given that his English isn't great, I think it's better to be safe than sorry.'

'Okay. I'll call the ambos,' Jet replied. 'Dutchy, see if you can explain to Tong and his mates what we're going to do and, Easy, you'd better get back out on the beach.'

'I'll get out of the way, too,' Poppy said to Jet. She knew the lifeguards could cope without her, they did it every day. 'I'll go for a swim and see you at Lily's for dinner.'

He nodded as he picked up the phone.

Ryder held the door for Poppy, letting her leave the tower before him. They walked down the metal stairs to the beach as Poppy tried to work out what Ryder was doing in Sydney. And why she was so nervous.

It was a silly reaction. They weren't teenagers any more. She didn't need to be nervous but apparently the old feelings of a first crush, a first love still simmered beneath the surface and didn't need much stirring to rise to the top.

Her mind wandered, skittering from past to present at a million miles an hour, taking her attention away from the simple task of walking down a staircase. She missed the bottom step and stumbled as the soft sand gave way beneath her. Before she had a chance to right herself Ryder's arm was around her waist, holding her, supporting her. Her top was loose, skimming the waistband of her shorts, and his fingers rested lightly on her skin. Her body buzzed under his touch, her skin tingled and her nerves endings sprang to life.

She found her feet and stepped away, forcing him to drop his arm, and then she found herself missing the contact.

What was the matter with her? she chided herself. She was a grown woman, in a relationship with another man. It was ridiculous to let a schoolgirl crush from a dozen years ago affect her like this.

But she couldn't help but wonder what it meant that Ryder's touch could still make her buzz when Craig's touch had never set her pulse racing, had never made her skin feel like it was on fire. But was that Craig's fault or hers?

She knew she deliberately sought out relationships that weren't based on an overpowering sense of physical desire. She didn't want a relationship that created huge emotional fluctuations for her. She chose calm and measured deliberately. It made her feel safe. She had chosen Craig because he had been able to give her the things she'd needed at the time. Was it his fault that what she had needed had been a place to call home more than a person to share it with? Was it Craig's fault that she didn't want to fall in love?

Her experience with Ryder had taught her that.

Falling in love had left her exposed and vulnerable. Now she didn't want to be emotionally dependent on someone. She didn't want to be needy. She didn't want to rely on anyone but herself.

Ryder had been her first love. Her only love. She'd tried to convince herself it had been nothing but a teenage crush but she'd known she was lying to herself. Falling in love had left her feeling foolish and rejected. He'd broken her heart and she'd vowed not to let herself fall in love again. And she'd kept her word.

But now, twelve years later, her head and her heart were sending conflicting messages. One touch, one smile and she was transported back to her teenage years when Ryder had been her world. When she'd thought he'd been the answer to her prayers. When he'd been the shining star in her small galaxy.

'Hop in, I'll give you a ride down the beach.' Even if his muscles were new, his voice was deep and familiar and it brought her out of her reverie and back to the present.

The open-sided lifeguard buggy was parked at the bottom of the stairs and Ryder had walked around to the driver's side and was sliding into his seat, oblivious to the simmering tension that was coursing through Poppy's body.

Her head was still spinning, still recovering from his touch. Unable to make decisions of her own, she followed his instructions and clambered into the buggy, stepping over the rescue board that was slotted along the side.

She stared at Ryder, still trying to process the idea that, A: he was here in Bondi, and B: her hormones were going crazy.

'What?' he said as she continued to look at him. 'Have I got something stuck on my face?' He grinned at her and wiped a hand down his cheek.

'No.' Poppy smiled in return. 'I'm still trying to get my head around the fact that you're here. Last I heard you were on the other side of the country, in Perth. I wasn't expecting to see you but you don't seem surprised to see me.'

'I'm not,' he said as he steered the buggy around a group of young girls sunbathing on the sand.

'You knew I was coming?'

'Daisy mentioned it.'

'Daisy did? You've seen her?'

'Of course. I've seen her at the beach and

I've been to dinner a few times with Jet at
Lily and Daisy's.'

She wondered why no one had said anything to her. She knew she tended to get
caught up in her own busy life but she was
sure no one had mentioned anything. She was
certain she would have remembered. Did they
assume she wouldn't be interested?

'In fact, Jet invited me to dinner tonight
too,' he continued.

'Are you coming?' she asked.

Ryder parked the buggy next to one of the
yellow signs that the lifeguards had posted
on the beach, warning swimmers of the dangerous currents. He shook his head as he hit
the kill switch and shut off the engine. 'No.'

She didn't know whether to be relieved or
disappointed. 'Are you busy?' She fished for
more information, even as she tried to tell
herself it didn't matter.

'No,' he explained. 'I thought you should
have some time with just the four of you.'

'Oh.' Now she knew she was disappointed.

'Maybe we could have dinner another time.
Catch up properly then.'

Her disappointment eased slightly. 'I'd like
that,' she said as she hopped out of the buggy.

Ryder had always been good company. So
often in her childhood she'd felt like she was

lost amongst the noise and chaos of her surroundings and she knew she'd developed a boisterous personality in an effort to be seen, to be noticed, but it hadn't done much good. Their family living arrangements had been unusual, and added to that growing up so close in age to her siblings meant everyone around the Carlson siblings treated them as one entity.

But Ryder hadn't. He'd always had time for her. He'd always listened to her. She'd struggled to find her own identity but he'd always seemed to see her, to understand her. She'd like to spend time with him. Provided she could get her nerves under control.

'I've got a couple of orientation days scheduled with the ambulance service, starting tomorrow,' she told him. 'Once I get my roster sorted, we can sort something out.'

Poppy smiled at him and then stepped out of her shorts and dropped them on the sand. He tried not to look as she lifted the hem of her T-shirt and pulled it over her head in one smooth movement to reveal a black bikini and toned abdominal muscles. She dropped her T-shirt onto her shorts and walked north along the beach towards the safer stretch of water. Away from the rip. Away from him.

He tried not to stare as she made her way into the water but it was his job to keep an eye on the swimmers and the ocean. He couldn't help it if she was in his field of vision. He watched her wade into the water, watched her until she dived under a small wave and struck out away from the beach.

He turned his attention back to the rest of the ocean, keeping an eye on the swimmers who weren't as confident in the water but he kept her in the periphery of his vision as his mind stayed focussed on her.

She was still gorgeous. Long, toned, athletic limbs, big, green eyes that seemed to hold the secrets of the universe, thick, blonde hair that fell in waves past her shoulders and perfect heart-shaped lips. Thinking about her lips reminded him of their kiss. In truth, he'd never forgotten it.

He'd been a lanky, gawky seventeen-year-old virgin. He'd had a couple of girlfriends, nothing serious, but Poppy had captivated him. Since the age of fifteen he'd had a thing for her but he'd never been confident enough to tell her so.

And then, out of the blue, she had kissed him.

He had no idea who she had kissed before him but it had been an amazing kiss. Like nothing he'd ever experienced. It had been incredible and unexpected.

They had spent a lot of time together over the years. He'd turned up often at the Carlson house under the guise of being Jet's best friend, but Poppy had been the real attraction. But she'd never given any sign that she was interested in him as anything other than a friend.

Until she'd kissed him.

And there'd only been one problem. She'd just been saying goodbye. His family had been moving away, four thousand kilometres away to the opposite side of the country. Poppy had hugged him first. She'd wrapped her slim arms around his even skinnier shoulders and told him she would miss him.

He'd said nothing. He'd been a teenage boy—he hadn't had the right words—and even if he had, the feeling of her embrace had left him speechless.

And then she'd kissed him and wiped all coherent thought from his young mind.

He'd been working on the courage to ask her out, finally deciding he needed to take the chance, before his world had imploded and the opportunity had been torn away from him by his mother's decision to pack up and move across the country. He'd figured he could have lived with that. It would have been a case of not knowing what he was missing but after she'd kissed him, after he'd had a taste of her, he'd known he would always rue the missed opportunity.

He hadn't wanted to leave. He hadn't wanted to leave *her*. But he'd had no choice. He'd had no valid reason to stay and his mother and his sister had needed him. Even as a teenage boy in love he'd been able to see that he had to go. Overnight he had become the man of the house and he'd had to do the right thing by his family. Especially considering that his father hadn't.

Eventually he'd got over the move. He'd got over the fact that he felt as if he'd been torn from Poppy's arms. And he'd got over the fact that his father's mid-life crisis—which had led him to run off with his much younger girlfriend—had instigated the change in his own circumstances. He'd even got over his parents' divorce, and eventually he'd got over the kiss too, but he'd never forgotten it.

He'd agonised over writing to Poppy, but he hadn't been any good with words. He'd been a seventeen-year-old boy who'd had no idea how to express what he'd been feeling, how *she* had made him feel, and so he'd said nothing, written nothing, and eventually the days had turned into weeks, which had turned into months, and all his thoughts had remained unspoken. And then it had been too late.

It had been the first kiss he'd had that had felt like it had had some meaning behind it, something shared, something emotional, rather than just something physical. It had become a moment in time, a moment in his history that had shaped him, and a moment he'd thought he'd put behind him, but now he was wondering what it would be like to kiss her again.

It was unlikely that he'd get that opportunity. He knew she had a partner, but it didn't mean he couldn't imagine what it would be like.

He kept his eyes on the water but his gaze kept drifting back to where Poppy was swimming.

He hadn't been surprised to see her as he'd been expecting her, but what he hadn't expected had been the sudden jolt of awareness when he'd seen her standing in the tower. He'd had the unsettling sensation of having the air knocked out of him. His pulse had been racing and it had felt as though his heart had suddenly got too big for his chest and had squeezed the air out of his lungs to make more room. He'd smiled and said hello and hoped he hadn't still sounded like the naïve, shy, tongue-tied teenager he'd been when he'd last seen her. But he suspected that he had.

She had become part of his past and he'd thought he'd got over her but seeing her again made it clear that there was still a connection. On his part at least.

He couldn't deny it was good to see her. Her clear green eyes still sparkled intensely, and when she looked at him, he felt as if he was the only person she was interested in seeing. He wondered if she made everyone feel that way.

Her smile still made the day brighter and her golden blonde hair still begged to be wound around his fingers. But, of course, he'd never done that. He'd never had the courage.

And he wouldn't dare to dream of doing it now either. He figured she'd probably forgotten all about him in the past twelve years and she'd no doubt kissed dozens of boys— men—in that time. She would have moved on and he wasn't about to remind her of their shared history. That would be far too embarrassing.

He would have liked to have accepted Jet's invitation to dinner tonight but he'd been uncertain. He'd been unsure if Poppy would want him there but his uncertainty had stemmed more from the fact he'd imagined that her boyfriend would be with her and he hadn't wanted to deal with that. He'd been prepared for the fact that she would be different from the girl he remembered but he hadn't been prepared to see her with another man. He'd known it would mess with his memories.

Ryder shook his head as he tried to clear his thoughts. Those memories needed to stay locked away for now—he had a job to do and he couldn't afford distractions. He swivelled his gaze up and down the shoreline. The beach was starting to empty as families went home for dinner and to prepare for the week ahead, but his attention was diverted by a woman who wasn't heading for the promenade but was hurrying towards him. By her side was a young boy who was holding a beach towel against his head.

'Can you have a look at my son, please? He collided with a boogie-boarder. He got a knee to the head and he has a cut by his eye.'

'Okay.' Ryder squatted down in the sand. 'Keep holding that towel there for a minute,' he said as it looked like the mother was about to move her son's hand. 'What's your name?'

'Jackson.'

'All right, Jackson, I'll just ask you a couple of questions and then I'll have a look at your battle wounds.' The boy had walked up to Ryder so he didn't appear to have sustained a spinal injury but Ryder would do a quick check just for his own peace of mind. He knew that one of the lifeguards had sustained a fractured thoracic vertebra in a collision in the water and it had gone undetected for a couple of days.

'Have you got any pain anywhere else?'

'No.'

'Any tingling or numbness in your fingers or toes?'

Jackson wriggled his toes in the sand. 'No.'

'Take a deep breath for me.' The boy closed his eyes as he followed Ryder's instructions, making Ryder concerned. 'How does that feel?'

'I feel a bit dizzy.'

Ryder knew that could be shock or concussion. 'All right, let's put you up here on the back of the buggy and I'll have a look.' He unzipped the first-aid kit while he was talking and then lifted the boy up onto the tray of the ATV before pulling on a pair of surgical gloves. He opened a packet of gauze and a vial of saline.

'Can you take the towel?' he asked Jackson's mother.

Once the wound was exposed Ryder poured

saline over the side of the boy's head to wash away the blood. Head wounds always bled a lot and often looked far worse than they actually were, but this cut had split the skin from the corner of Jackson's left eye halfway to his temple. There was a bruise forming already. He'd been knocked hard but the cut wasn't deep.

Ryder taped a wad of gauze over the wound. 'I think we'll take you up to the tower to patch you up properly. You can hop up here with him,' he told the mother. 'I'll drive you back slowly.'

Ryder got Jackson back to the tower and up the stairs. He laid him on the treatment bed and slid the oxygen mask over the boy's nose and mouth, knowing that would help if he was in shock. He draped a space blanket over him to counteract the heat loss from his wet bathing shorts.

'Can you tell me what day it is, Jackson?' Ryder asked as he removed the wad of bloodied gauze.

'Sunday. Does this mean I can stay home from school tomorrow?'

'I reckon you deserve a day off,' Ryder told him. Jackson was going to look battered and bruised by tomorrow and would probably feel pretty tender.

Ryder managed to stem the flow of blood but Jackson was going to need more help than he was qualified to give him in order to close the wound.

'All right. The cut's not too deep but I reckon we'll get the ambos to have a look at it.' The cut was a couple of centimetres long and being close to the eye Ryder thought it was better to err on the side of caution.

'Will it need stitches?' Jackson's mother asked.

'I think they'll be able to glue the edges closed. That will mean no swimming for a week but he can have a quick shower in twenty-four hours.'

'So he's okay?'

'The ambos will do a more thorough check but it seems like he's come out of this without too much trouble, but if he gets a temperature in the next day or has any nausea or dizziness you'll need to take him to your local doctor.'

'Okay, thank you.'

Jet called the ambulance for the second time that day and Ryder left his patient in the care of the lifeguards in the tower. He needed to get back out onto the sand as it was time to start packing up.

The beach was patrolled from six in the morning until seven at night. The lifeguards

worked staggered shifts with a maximum
of eight on at a time, but because it wasn't
yet peak season more than half had finished
work, leaving skeleton staff to close the beach
at the end of the day.

Ryder took the buggy and drove along the
sand, pulling up the yellow warning signs,
picking up cones and bringing in the flags.
He pulled out the dangerous-current sign
where Poppy had left her clothes.

Her clothes were gone.

He checked the beach but she was nowhere
to be seen.

She hadn't said goodbye but, then, why
would she? He consoled himself with the
knowledge that at least it wouldn't be another
twelve years until he saw her again.

Poppy towelled herself dry after a quick
shower. The house had been empty when
she'd got back from the beach but she could
hear noise coming from the kitchen and she
knew at least one of her sisters was home
from the hospital. She rifled through her bag
and found some clean underwear and a light
cotton sundress. She got dressed and headed
for the kitchen.

Her little sister, Daisy, was sliding a tray
into the oven as Poppy walked in. She had her

back to Poppy but when she straightened and turned, she had a big smile on her pretty face.

'I thought I'd be able to sneak up on you.' Poppy laughed before she stepped forward and hugged her tightly.

'You should know better than that. You've just got out of the shower. You smell fresh.'

'That's good to know.' Poppy smiled.

Daisy was completely deaf, having lost her hearing at the age of eight after contracting mumps. Because she had already been talking her speech was mostly unaffected by her hearing loss. She could lip read and sign, which gave her good communication options, provided she could see people's faces.

'What's for dinner?' Poppy asked.

'Baked snapper with baby potatoes. You can make a salad if you like.'

Poppy pulled a bottle of wine and salad ingredients from the fridge. She poured two glasses of wine, passing one to her sister, and then made sure she was standing at the kitchen bench, facing Daisy, before she continued their conversation.

'How was work?'

Daisy screwed up her nose. 'I don't think the nurse unit manager likes me.'

'Why not?' Poppy was flummoxed. *Every-one* liked Daisy.

Daisy was tiny, blonde, blue-eyed and beautiful—she reminded Poppy of a fairy—and people were naturally drawn to her. Almost everyone wanted to be her best friend, which was ironic as Daisy was quite happy with her own company. Daisy had been born a twin but the infection that had robbed her of her hearing had also claimed the life of her twin sister, Willow, and after that Daisy, who had only ever needed Willow's company, had retreated into her shell. She'd been mothered by her older siblings but because of the five-year age difference between Poppy and Daisy she had spent a lot of time on her own.

She was quiet and introverted but in the field of paediatric nursing she had found the place she felt comfortable. She loved working with kids—they were uncomplicated—and Daisy adored them and they her. Poppy knew Daisy would be completely happy if she could work with kids and never have to see an adult but even if Daisy didn't need adult company, it was rare for someone to take objection to her.

'What happened?' Poppy asked, wondering what could have gone wrong.

'It might have something to do with something she heard me say.'

Poppy didn't like to talk about her feel-

ings but none of the Carlson siblings had
any qualms about voicing their opinions on
other matters. Even Lily and Daisy, the 'quiet'
ones, weren't afraid to let people know their
thoughts on general topics if it was something
they felt strongly about. Along with their fair
athletic looks the four of them shared determined natures and opinionated views.

'Which was?'

'We admitted a child today who has a serious case of chicken pox with several compli-
cations and I might have strongly suggested
to her parents that there is a vaccine for this
disease and they should consider vaccinating
their children.'

'And what did the NUM say?'

'She told me it's not my place to lecture
the parents.'

'She's probably right.'

Daisy sighed. 'I know. But I had no idea
she was standing right behind me.'

'Would you have modified your lecture if
you had known?'

'No. You know there are laws in New
South Wales about vaccinating children unless there's a medical reason not to? If it's
good enough for the government it's good
enough for me.'

'That sounds like a serious discussion be-

tween two of my favourite sisters,' Jet said
as he walked into the kitchen. 'What have I
missed?'

'Daisy's been lecturing people about vaccinations again,' Poppy said with a smile.

'It's hard for me to keep quiet,' Daisy pro-
tested. 'I'm a walking advertisement for why
vaccinations are so important.'

Jet gave her a quick hug on his way to the
fridge. 'Yes, you are, Daise, stick to your
guns.'

'I intend to.'

'Good for you,' he said as he helped himself to a beer and flipped the top off the bottle. He turned towards Poppy. 'How was your
swim? Cleared the cobwebs out after your
road trip?'

Poppy nodded.

'Craig didn't change his mind and come
with you?' he asked.

'No. He was busy,' Poppy replied.

'Busy with what?'

Other than his work she wasn't exactly sure
what he was busy doing. They hadn't spent a
lot of time together lately. They never really
did. Their relationship wasn't one where they
spent every spare minute together and that
was the way Poppy liked it. She suspected
she'd grow tired of Craig if they lived in each

other's pockets. Craig didn't need to spend every second with her or hear how she felt about him constantly and the same went for her. They had a compatible partnership even if they didn't rely on each other emotionally.

They were working towards a common goal and that was enough for Poppy. With Craig's help she was going to achieve the financial and physical stability and security she craved much faster. With Craig's help she would pay off a mortgage and own a house.

For her part she'd been volunteering for any overtime shifts that had been offered, trying to save as much money as she could—working extra weekends and nights while Craig had worked days. 'Making money, I hope. We have to get our house finished.'

'I need to see this house. With the amount of money you seem to be throwing at it, I'm imagining something along the lines of the Taj Mahal by the time you're finished.'

Poppy laughed. 'It's nothing extravagant but I wanted to modernise it without losing the heritage feeling, and everything with a Queenslander seems to cost more.' The typical Queenslander house, built out of wood and raised off the ground on stilts, required a lot of TLC and a lot of cash if it had fallen into disrepair. Poppy and Craig had spent huge amounts on things that couldn't be seen—replacing beams and joists and panels in the frame, the walls and the floors, as well as re-wiring the house, and they weren't done yet. The bathroom and laundry had recently been completed but the kitchen needed updating, the pool needed landscaping, and there was always wood that needed painting.

'Would you do it again? Renovate?'

'I don't know about "again,"' she said, as Lily joined them and Daisy took the snapper from the oven. 'It's not like we've even finished one yet. It's been a lot of effort.' On her part more than Craig's, she thought, but she didn't say that out loud. Craig put money into the house but she was the one who had the ideas, organised the tradesmen and picked up a paintbrush. To Craig the house was a sound investment but it was more than that to Poppy.

The house was her sanctuary and she loved the restoration process. She loved seeing her plans come to fruition, bringing the house back to life, but Craig had frequently re-minded her not to get too attached. He looked at the house as an investment, his goal was purely financial. His aim was to renovate and sell for a profit and she knew she'd agreed to those plans in the beginning but the house had come to represent more than just dollars to her. It was her chance to have a home.

Initially she had seen the house as her path to financial security but during the renovation process it had come to represent physical security too. The house was a place she could call her own, and one that she had control over. She didn't want to pay someone else's mortgage. She didn't want to be at someone else's mercy. She didn't want to be a tenant, always hoping that she would be able to stay. She wanted a place of her own. One she couldn't be moved out of without her consent. She wanted security and stability and she was prepared to work hard to get it.

The house represented those things and she hoped that once the house was finished Craig would love it as much as she did and agree to keep it.

'I'd like to propose a toast,' Lily said as they sat down to dinner. 'To the four of us being together again.'

'It's been much too long,' Daisy added as they raised their glasses.

Poppy knew that was her fault. Her siblings had dinner together regularly, it was she who had been missing. She'd spent every spare minute on her goals. Every spare day either doing an extra shift or wielding a hammer, screwdriver or paintbrush. She hadn't wanted to spend the time or the money on trips to Sydney. Looking around the table now, she was sorry that she hadn't made more of an effort but she consoled herself with the knowledge that it would all be worth it in the end, once her house was finished.

'It's good to be here,' she said, 'and I'd like to think we'll be able to have family dinner at my house next year.'

'Maybe we could have Christmas in Brisbane,' Daisy suggested.

'Speaking of Christmas...' The others laughed as Lily spoke up. She never missed an opportunity to organise them. 'Will everyone be in Sydney this year?'

Christmas had only become an event for the Carlson siblings in the past half a dozen years. They had grown up in a commune in Byron Bay. They'd had an unusual childhood and traditions had been non-existent. Birthdays, graduations, Christmas, none of those had been considered remarkable or special in any way. No fuss had ever been made about an event, no child had ever been singled out as anything or anyone special, no achievement ever congratulated. It had only been when the four of them had begun to spread their wings and experienced how other families celebrated that they had begun to have more traditional celebrations, and that had included Christmas.

Lily organised Christmas get-togethers now. She had adopted her husband's traditions with family gathered around the table for lunch followed by a swim at the beach or in the pool in the afternoon. But Otto had been in London last Christmas and Lily had spent the day with her own siblings. Poppy wondered where Otto would be this year.

'I'll be here,' Poppy said. 'I won't have any leave.'

She hadn't discussed Christmas plans with Craig. They'd spent last Christmas in Sydney on a brief visit, which meant it was probably her turn to spend Christmas with his family, but she knew she'd rather spend it with hers. She'd had one Christmas with his family and she'd felt like a fish out of water. It had been strange. Her discomfort hadn't been specifically related to Christmas, she had never felt like a good fit with them. She still felt like an outsider, always hovering on the edges. She knew she was to blame—she didn't want to get too involved. She didn't want to be rejected.

The dinner conversation was robust as they caught up on everything from work to books

they'd enjoyed to Jet's love life and training schedule, but as the evening progressed
Poppy found she was more interested in the
topics that weren't being discussed—no one
had mentioned Otto and no one had mentioned Ryder either.

She wondered where Ryder would be for
Christmas. Was his move to Sydney permanent? Were his family still in Perth? But
she didn't want to bring Ryder's name up in
front of her sisters, she didn't want to draw
attention to her interest. She knew her sisters
would ask probing questions that she wouldn't
have the answers to.

As the eldest sibling, Lily was the organ-
iser. She was the writer of lists and the one
who made sure they all kept in touch. Lily
had a strong protective nature, an inherent
desire to look out for her siblings. She would
want to know all the details and Poppy wasn't
ready to divulge anything just yet. If ever.

Daisy was the dreamer, seemingly content
in her own world and, being deaf, it was too
easy for her to ignore everyone and everything going on around her. But Daisy was
also the romantic in the family and Poppy
knew she would start to imagine all sorts of
starry-eyed scenarios and Poppy wasn't sure

that was where she wanted the conversation to head.

She decided to wait for a chance to speak to Jet alone, he'd be the least likely to wonder about her questions. He wouldn't analyse her comments, he'd take them at face value and answer in his usual straightforward manner with no additional cross-examination.

When Jet offered to do the dishes, Poppy saw her opportunity and volunteered to help.

'I didn't realise Ryder was in Bondi,' she said as she filled the sink with water. 'What's he doing here?' She asked the question that had been on the tip of her tongue all night.

'He's been travelling around Australia on a bit of a gap year.'

'How did he end up working with you? I thought it was pretty competitive to get work at Bondi.' Not to mention requiring a high skill level.

'We're down a couple of lifeguards because of injuries and Easy's been working as a lifeguard at Cottesloe Beach in Perth so the council offered him a casual position to fill the gaps over summer, just until the others are fit again.'

'He's a professional lifeguard?' Poppy knew that the paid lifeguard jobs were coveted. The job was demanding, challenging and rewarding but, in Poppy's opinion, not remunerated adequately given the level of responsibility the lifeguards had and the hours they worked, and she couldn't imagine that anyone would plan on being a lifeguard for ever. She knew there were plenty of lifeguards who had been in the job for years but she, privately, thought they should be aspiring to more. She thought *Ryder* should be aspiring to more but, for once, she kept her opinion to herself, knowing it said more about her than about Ryder.

As Poppy collapsed into bed at the end of a hectic but fabulous day her phone beeped, alerting her to a missed call from Craig. She crawled under the covers and rang him back.

'Hi, sorry I missed your call,' she said, even as she wondered why she was apologising. He was the one who had let her calls go unanswered. But she tried to rein in her irritation. It wasn't like Craig to be uncontactable. He was consistent. Safe. Predictable. He rarely turned his phone off. Doing so was out of character for him and she found it unsettling. 'Is everything okay?'

'Yes, everything's fine. I've just got home from golf.'

'At nine o'clock at night?'

'I stayed for dinner at the club.'

Her irritation rose to the surface again. There were a dozen tasks that that needed to be completed on the house and while some of those things required professional, skilled tradespeople, other jobs could be done by her and Craig. He could have been wielding a paintbrush instead of a golf club today. He could have been returning her calls instead of dining out.

'You didn't start the painting?' She was annoyed now and she could hear the abruptness in her tone but she couldn't temper it.

'No. I don't see much point when there's still work to be done inside,' he replied. 'The kitchen, the deck, those bifold doors need to be installed. We can get painters in once everything is finished.'

Who was going to pay for that? Poppy wondered. She knew that some of the painting would have to be done by professionals, scaffolding would need to be set up to do the exterior, but they'd agreed that they would tackle some of the internal painting themselves to save money.

All Poppy could see was dollars. She'd been working overtime, taking every extra shift that was offered to her, in order to save the money needed to finish their house. Surely Craig could do his bit rather than take a day off to play golf?

CHAPTER THREE

RYDER SAT IN the lifeguard tower and monitored the beach. He alternated between peering through the binoculars, scanning the beach with his naked eyes and checking the monitors that displayed the feeds from the cameras installed along the promenade, looking for anything untoward.

He was currently volunteering for every available shift. He wanted to be busy, he wanted to keep his *mind* busy. He'd spent far too much time over the past several days thinking about Poppy and wondering how her first shifts had gone, and it was time he focussed on something else.

He hadn't seen her for twelve years and he'd managed to get through each day without thinking about her constantly but now that he had seen her again he couldn't get her out of his head.

It was ridiculous. He was ridiculous. Sitting here like a lovestruck teenager.

After a dozen years she couldn't possibly still be the same girl he'd once known. Once loved. But try telling his heart that. The minute he'd laid eyes on her again he'd been knocked for six. His heart had started racing, leaving him so short of breath he'd felt as if he'd just completed the physically torturous, gruelling lifeguard challenge.

But it didn't matter how he felt or what he thought. She was dating another guy. In an adult world that didn't leave room for him.

They could only be friends. He knew they couldn't go back to their teenage years, back to their first kiss, but he couldn't stop himself from wishing for more.

A knock on the tower door brought him out of the past. He jumped up from his seat before anyone else had even moved, eager to answer the call, eager to have something to occupy his time and his mind.

He opened the door to find a couple of teenagers pacing on the threshold. He could tell they had come from the skate park. They weren't wearing boardshorts, they were wearing shoes and shirts with their shorts and were dressed predominantly in black despite the warm weather.

'Hey, boys, what's the problem?'

'Our friend came off his skateboard.'

Bingo.

'He hit his head. He seems pretty bad.'

Attending to incidents on the beach or in the ocean were only part of the lifeguards' duties. As council employees they also responded to incidents in other council areas like the skate park, the roads and footpaths or the area around the Bondi Pavilion building. Because the ambos had to come from the station near the hospital while the lifeguards were on location, on some days they seemed to spend just as much time assisting off the beach as they did on it. Mostly that wasn't an issue, only becoming problematic when there were several incidents at once that took multiple lifeguards away from the beach. Or when one incident required several lifeguards to attend.

Ryder grabbed a kit bag and a radio. 'I've got this one, Gibbo,' he said over his shoulder. 'Can you send someone with the spinal board to back me up?' It would be faster for the larger equipment to follow Ryder but he knew he needed it on hand. The risk of head or spinal injuries was high in the skate bowl.

The skate park was three hundred metres south of the tower, overlooking the beach.

Ryder slung the kit bag over his shoulder and set out. The boys kept pace with him as he ran along the promenade.

The skate park was large with several different areas catering for differing levels of abilities. There were grommets on scooters and boards in the gentler areas but no one was skating in the bowl. Ryder looked over the edge and saw several boarders clustered around a prostrate figure on the ground. He stepped over the lip and down into the bowl.

The skate park was baking in the sun. The concrete bowl soaked up the heat and there was no shade to offer any protection. The blue-painted concrete was hot under his bare feet but he knew from experience that he wouldn't notice in a minute.

He slid the first-aid kit from his shoulder and squatted down beside the injured teenager. His eyes were closed. His face was ashen and a sheen of sweat coated his skin.

'What's his name?'

'Connor.'

'Connor, can you hear me? My name's Ryder, I'm a lifeguard, come to check you out.'

Connor opened his eyes. Ryder thought his pupils were a little sluggish to react to the light and the left one appeared slightly more dilated. But at least he was conscious.

Ryder surveyed their surroundings. A skateboard lay by Connor's side but Ryder couldn't see any protective equipment. 'Was he wearing a helmet?' he asked.

'No.'

He held back a sigh, wondering when these kids would learn. He'd seen the tricks they attempted, he'd seen how hard they fell and he'd seen the injuries they'd sustained and he knew they'd seen them too. But so many of them still seemed to think they were invincible. The delusions of youth, he thought. If he had a dollar for every young boy who needed help on the beach or in the skate park he'd be a rich man. Ryder wasn't sure if it was due to a lack of concentration, a lack of judgement, a lack of awareness of the consequences of their actions or just an increased attraction to risky activities, or all of them, but it was almost always the boys getting into strife.

He focussed on his patient. Connor had a suspected head injury and an obvious fracture of his left lower leg. His foot was at an awkward angle and Ryder knew he would be in immense pain. He wouldn't be climbing out of the bowl. But before he could be moved Ryder needed to check for any additional injuries, especially spinal. He radioed for the tower to request an ambulance and started his assessment while he waited for back-up.

'Other than your leg, does it hurt anywhere else?'

'My head.' Connor's voice was faint and Ryder suspected the pain was making him feel sick.

'Can you tell me what day it is?'

'Saturday?'

It was Wednesday. After school.

'Are you allergic to anything?' Ryder asked while he checked Connor's wrist and neck, looking for any allergy alerts. He wasn't convinced he could take Connor's word for it given his condition but there was no sign of any medic alert necklace or bracelet or anything to indicate he had a pre-existing medical condition.

He opened his kit bag and prepared some pain relief. Getting Connor out of the skate bowl was going to hurt.

He handed him the little green inhaler. 'Breathe through the inhaler, mate. That'll settle the pain a bit before we get you out of here.'

Six or seven breaths would effectively kickstart the pain relief and make it possible to move him without causing too much more

discomfort. By the time Gibbo and Dutchy
arrived with the spinal board Ryder had satisfied himself that Connor hadn't sustained
a spinal injury and the pain relief had begun
to work.

'The ambos are on the way,' Dutchy said
as he slid down into the bowl.

Ryder nodded in response before giving
them a summary of Connor's history. 'We
need to splint his leg, stabilise his neck as a
precaution and get him out of the bowl and
into the shade,' he said in conclusion.

He spoke to Connor. 'How are you feeling
now, mate? Is that whistle doing the trick?'

Connor grinned and stuck up one thumb.
The pain relief was having the desired effect
but Ryder knew the move would still be uncomfortable.

'Good stuff. We're going to stabilise you
and carry you out of here ready for the ambos.
It'll probably hurt a bit. Just keep hold of that
whistle and suck on it when you need to.'

The green whistle was good for about half
an hour of pain relief, which would be enough
to cover Connor until the paramedics arrived
and could give him something stronger if
needed.

Ryder and Dutchy wrapped a cervical
collar around Connor's neck before sliding

a splint made of thick cardboard onto the boy's leg. Ryder added some padding, filling in the gaps, before taping it in position. Once Connor's injuries were suitably protected, they rolled him while Gibbo positioned the stretcher. They secured Connor on the stretcher and lifted him gently. Ryder could hear the sirens of the approaching ambulance as the three lifeguards hoisted their patient carefully out of the bowl. They carried him over the hot pavement to a shady spot where the ambos would have access and laid him on the ground.

The ambulance pulled to a stop beside them. The siren was silenced, although the lights continued to flash. Ryder recognised Alex as he climbed out of the ambulance and went to open the rear doors. Poppy climbed out of the driver's seat and walked towards Ryder.

He couldn't help but notice how good she looked. The uniforms were not usually flattering but hers looked as though it had been custom fitted. Her pants were belted, showing off her narrow waist, and the fabric hugged her hips and thighs and drew his attention to the curve of her bottom. The normally unbecoming uniform did nothing to hide Poppy's sensational figure.

'Hey, what have we got?' she asked as she squatted beside him.

Ryder redirected his gaze and his mind and returned his focus to their patient. 'This is Connor, fifteen-year-old male, who came off second best in a battle with the bowl. He has a fractured left lower leg and he's a bit confused. He wasn't wearing a helmet so he's likely concussed and may possibly have a head injury.'

He was still in a lot of pain, gripping tightly to the green whistle.

Poppy nodded before speaking to Connor. 'Hi, Connor. I'm Poppy, a paramedic. I'm going to have a look at you and then I reckon we'll go for a ride to the hospital.'

'Can you close your eyes for me, Connor? Keep them closed,' she said as he followed her instructions, 'I'll open them for you, one at a time, okay?'

Poppy took a small torch from one of her many pockets and pointed it at Connor's cheek. She lifted one of his eyelids and flicked the torchlight over his eye, watching for a reaction, before repeating the test on the other eye.

She then repeated the tests Ryder had done for a possible spinal injury and once she agreed with his assessment and cleared him of anything serious they transferred him to the ambulance stretcher, still taking care to support his head.

'Do you want to change the splint on his leg?' Ryder asked.

Poppy shook her head. 'No. That seems secure and stable enough. It will just cause more discomfort if we change it. Bondi General is only a few minutes' drive away.'

Ryder watched as Poppy inserted a cannula into the back of Connor's hand, ready for more pain relief if needed, and slipped an oxygen mask over his nose and mouth to help with shock.

'Has his family been notified?' she asked as she and Alex raised the stretcher up on its legs.

'Not yet. I'll speak to his mates and sort that out. I'll get someone to meet him at the hospital.'

Poppy nodded as she loaded Connor into the back of the ambulance. She climbed into the driver's seat and Ryder watched as she drove away.

He returned to work but having seen Poppy he now found it harder than ever to keep his thoughts on track. He smiled. Maybe he was still more like those teenage boys than he wanted to admit. Lacking concentration and easily distracted. He didn't want to think he was attracted to risky activities but what else could he call being fixated on another man's girlfriend? He didn't need his degree in psychology to know it was a mistake. This was a situation that was never going to end well for him.

Poppy threw her sandwich wrapper in the bin and checked her watch. She and Alex were taking a late meal break on Campbell Parade but she had time to duck across to the tower. She knew the lifeguards liked to hear updates on their patients but she also knew it wasn't absolutely necessary and she was using Connor's accident as an excuse to see Ryder.

She knocked on the door.

The lifeguard who opened the door was halfway through pulling his shirt on but even though his face was obscured she knew it was Ryder. She was trained to be observant and after the other day she'd recognise his naked chest and ripped abdominal muscles anywhere. The image was permanently imprinted on her brain. She let go of her disappointment as his shirt covered up her view.

'Hey.' He smiled at her and her stomach fluttered.

'Hi,' she said. 'I was just grabbing something to eat across the road and thought I'd update you on Connor.'

'Any dramas?'

Poppy shook her head. 'Not really. He was lucky. He had a simple fracture of his left tib and fib, as you know, but they also picked up a hairline fracture of his skull. Nothing that he won't make a full recovery from, though, so that's a plus.'

Ryder grinned and said, 'Maybe next time he'll wear a helmet.'

'Maybe. But even if he does you and I both know there will be plenty more just like him. Plenty of kids who take risks. We see it every day.'

'I know. The invincibility of youth. But I don't suppose we can blame them really—we weren't so different. You were pretty wild.' Ryder laughed.

'I blame Jet.' She smiled. 'And you were a part of it, too.'

Life in the commune on the outskirts of Byron Bay had been largely unsupervised. The adults in the commune had professed not to believe in structured learning, firm discipline or strict supervision, and Poppy and Jet along with a band of mischievous childhood friends, including Ryder, had spent their time running wild in the bush, jumping off the rocks into the ocean with their surfboards and generally creating chaos.

Poppy's mother had worked in the general store and had dabbled in natural therapies and healing and her father had run a surf school, but while he had taught the children to surf they had mostly been left to their own devices and, to all intents and purposes, had virtually raised themselves. She hadn't minded as a teenager but as she'd matured she'd wondered if her parents' way of raising a family had been the best. She'd known they'd thought they were free from social norms but she actually would have liked some more attention and had probably needed a few more boundaries.

Lily had been the voice of reason, the one Poppy hadn't wanted to disappoint, the one she'd looked up to, who'd set an example for the rest of them. She often wondered where she would be today if she hadn't had Lily's sensible, calming influence. 'I'm not sure that my childhood should be held up as an example of what is desirable,' she said.

She had been in the thick of things but she hadn't really been a huge risk-taker. She'd only joined in because Ryder had been part of the group. Jumping into the ocean to go surfing had been no hardship, she would have walked over hot coals for him.

'Maybe not, but I think you turned out okay.'

He smiled and she felt the old, familiar sense of connection. The one she had only ever felt with him. It was strange that after almost a dozen years she still had the sense that they were close. The sense that he knew her, that he truly understood her.

He was leaning against the doorjamb, close enough to touch. She wanted to touch him. She wanted to slide her hand under his shirt and place her palm over his heart. She wanted to feel his skin under hers.

She clenched her hand into a fist at her side to stop herself from doing anything unwise. Maybe they could still be friends but she knew she couldn't hope for anything more.

To her right she saw Bluey jogging up the stairs from the beach. As Ryder moved to give him room to enter the tower, he stepped towards her and she caught her breath as his movement brought him even further into her space. His leg brushed against her hip and she waited for him to move away once Bluey had passed by, but he stayed in the doorway, connected to her.

She could smell him now. He smelt like the

ocean, salty and warm, and she realised he must have been into the sea since she'd seen him earlier in the afternoon.

She inhaled his scent as she tilted her head and looked up into his blue eyes.

He was watching her, his gaze intense.

All she had to do was reach for him.

She wanted to pull his head towards hers, pull his mouth to hers, press her lips against his and kiss him again. Like she'd done twelve years before.

But she couldn't.

Those days were gone.

They could only be friends.

She knew once upon a time she'd wanted more but they had both moved on.

She took a step back, a half-step really, just enough to break their physical connection, enough to break the spell he seemed to have cast over her, enough to let her breathe again.

'Have you got plans for tonight?' he asked. 'Do you want to grab a bite to eat?'

Her heart leapt before she remembered that she did have plans. Disappointment flooded through her. 'I can't. Daisy and I are going to see a movie at the Italian film festival.' Foreign films were Daisy's favourite, the subtitles made them the perfect choice for her. Poppy wondered briefly if he'd like to come with them but she didn't want to extend the invitation without checking with Daisy first.

'How about some time over the weekend, then?'

She shook her head. 'That's no good either. Craig is coming to town, we're looking at properties to rent.' As was her way, if she wasn't working, she had filled any gaps in her schedule with other activities. She liked to be busy and with Craig coming to Sydney as well she had no spare time. But she hoped he wouldn't think she was avoiding him. She wanted to make sure they kept or rekindled their friendship. He was still important to her. 'Can I take a rain check?'

Poppy and Daisy lay on their surfboards and let Backpackers' Rip carry them out past the breaking waves. The rip might create problems for unsuspecting swimmers and cause no end of headaches for the Bondi lifeguards but for the surfers it acted as a highway, carrying them out to sea and letting them save their energy. Using the power of the water meant there was no need to paddle hard to get out the back.

The Carlson siblings had surfed all their lives. Growing up in Byron Bay and having a father who was a surf instructor and ex-professional surfer had meant they had been put on boards almost the moment they could stand. Poppy hadn't surfed for almost a year, since the last time she'd been to Bondi. She hadn't even brought her board down with her on this trip but had borrowed one from Lily.

Lily hadn't used her board for months either and had declined to come with them today. Poppy was enjoying surfing with Daisy but next time she'd insist that Lily come too. There was no better way to free your mind than to paddle out into the ocean, thinking only about what the water was doing, about the next wave. The freedom of riding a wave into shore was exhilarating and Poppy was pretty sure Lily could use some time to clear her head. It was like riding a bike—she wouldn't have lost her skills, she just needed to commit the time.

Poppy needed to clear her mind too. She was irritated and she knew the ocean would help to calm her down. She had spent hours over the past couple of weeks looking at potential rental properties in anticipation of Craig's visit. She had lined up three properties to view only to find out—when she'd called him to check his flight details—that he'd cancelled his trip to Sydney for the weekend as he was snowed under at work.

Subsequently, she'd cancelled the appointments to view two of the potential rentals in Surry Hills, which was Craig's preferred suburb. She wasn't prepared to waste her time looking at properties she didn't want to live in. She justified the cancellations by telling herself that Craig was fussy and the rental property market was competitive. She knew the agent would want to meet both of them and that the properties were likely to be snapped up before Craig got to Sydney.

Poppy wanted to live near Bondi—she was the one who would be coming and going in the dark. She wanted to be close to work and near the beach, whereas Craig wanted to be closer to the city. He didn't want to tackle the rush-hour commute but given that he usually worked from eight in the morning until six she figured he'd miss the heaviest traffic. She'd gone alone to look at the one property she'd earmarked in Bondi but it was small and gloomy, a bit depressing really, and she'd reluctantly crossed it off her list.

Now, as she sat on her board out beyond the break, waiting for her turn on a wave, she tried to quash her irritation at Craig and her wasted afternoon. She wasn't annoyed about not seeing Craig but she was annoyed by the inconvenience and the time she'd wasted.

What sort of person did that make her? That she wasn't upset about not seeing her boyfriend? What was wrong with her?

She knew exactly what was wrong.

Ryder.

She couldn't get him out of her head.

She wasn't missing Craig and she wasn't desperate to see him, they didn't have that sort of relationship. She didn't depend on him emotionally and she knew he didn't depend on her. Which was how she liked it. She didn't want to rely on Craig for love and affection. She could get hurt that way.

But she'd barely even thought about Craig over the past few days, she'd been too busy thinking about Ryder. And sex. Which was another unfamiliar pastime for her. Sex wasn't high on her list of priorities. Sure, she felt the need for it occasionally but since seeing Ryder again she'd found herself thinking about it constantly. Thinking about being in his arms, touching him, making love to him.

Her hormones had gone into overdrive—just like when she'd first fallen for him as a teenager.

Ryder was an idea that had remained trapped in the depths of her psyche. She had relegated him to her past and closed that part of herself off, the part that had loved him. She hadn't wanted to love again, it was too painful, but seeing him again had awoken those memories with a vengeance.

He was an itch that had never been scratched.

But she knew it was more than that. Something about him still made her heart sing. She felt a sense of anticipation and excitement when he was near. He still fascinated her. She needed to be careful.

The light was beginning to fade as the day drifted towards dusk and the last of the beachgoers started to make their way home. There were a few other surfers in the water but not many swimmers. The day had been overcast and a storm was threatening. Thunder rumbled in the distance. The storm was getting closer and Poppy knew they'd have to call it a day before the weather turned nasty. The ocean was not an ideal spot to be in an electrical storm.

Daisy was on her board beside her and she turned her head as a burst of lightning lit up the sky to the north. Daisy wouldn't have heard the thunder but the bright flash of light was enough to catch her attention.

Surfers around them began to catch waves in to the beach as another lightning bolt crackled to their right. It was close. Poppy signalled to Daisy that they should follow suit as a thunderclap crashed overhead. A set was rolling in and they waited their turn before catching a wave behind another pair of surfers.

Poppy could feel the static electricity in the air as they hit the shore and she had just picked her board up out of the water when lightning flashed in front of her. It was so bright she turned her head to block the light. She heard the damp sand sizzle where one fork of lightning struck the beach and the ground trembled beneath her feet.

A second fork arced between the sky and the earth but this one didn't reach the sand. Poppy watched in horror as it hit one of the men who had surfed in on the wave before Daisy and her. He was still in the shallow water and the strike knocked him off his feet and threw him through the air.

He landed on his back, facing the sky.

Poppy and Daisy ripped off their leg ropes, dropped their boards and sprinted towards the man.

The man's wetsuit had a hole just below his right shoulder, a couple of inches in from his armpit, and Poppy knew that was the point of contact. His eyes were closed and he wasn't breathing.

The smell of burnt flesh made bile rise up in her throat.

She crouched down beside him and put her fingers on his wrist, searching for a pulse. Nothing.

The man was lying on damp sand, surrounded by a few centimetres of water. Poppy knew the tide was turning and the air was still charged with electricity. She didn't want to administer first aid in the water during a thunderstorm. His mate was beside him, sitting completely still, doing nothing, obviously in shock, looking dazedly from Poppy and Daisy back to the unconscious surfer.

'Grab him under his arms,' she said to his mate, 'We need to drag him out of the water.'

She grabbed the man's feet and they pulled him out of the shallows and moved him higher up the beach onto drier sand.

'What's his name?' she asked as they'd got him to semi-safety and she knelt again in the sand.

'Scotty.' The man still looked dazed but at least he was able to respond to her questions and instructions. 'He's my brother. Is he going to be okay?'

'I don't know,' she said. There was no way of sugar-coating the facts. She held Scotty's wrist and felt again for a pulse as she watched for any slight rise and fall of his chest to indicate that he was breathing. 'Do you know how to do CPR?' she asked the patient's brother.

'Kind of.'

'I'm a paramedic. Follow my instructions and we'll do our best until the lifeguards get here, okay?'

Scotty still wasn't breathing. Out of habit she shook his shoulder gently to see if she could rouse him. 'Scotty? Can you hear me?'

There was no sign of life.

Daisy was kneeling next to Poppy. She opened Scotty's mouth and checked that his tongue wasn't blocking his airway. She gripped him under the chin.

'I need you to do the breaths for me,' she told the man. Daisy was a nurse, trained in CPR, but she didn't want to expose Daisy to any risk. If Scotty's brother was competent with the breaths, that was Poppy's preferred option. She would do the compressions—they were the most important thing at this stage. 'Hold his head back like Daisy is doing and breathe for him when I tell you,' she said.

The man nodded and Poppy signed instructions to Daisy, telling her to make sure the lifeguards were on their way, as she started chest compressions. 'I'll count to thirty and then stop while you give two breaths, okay?'

She'd started on the third round of compressions before she heard the lifeguard buggy pull up beside them. It felt like ten minutes, not one.

She turned her head and saw Ryder and Dutchy jump out of the buggy. She didn't think she'd ever been as pleased to see Ryder.

'Lightning strike,' she told them she continued counting in her head. 'We're going to need the defib.'

Ryder nodded and turned back to lift the defibrillator bag from the buggy as Dutchy dropped the kit bag in the sand and pulled a pair of scissors from it. Poppy sat back on the count of thirty and instructed Scotty's brother to give two breaths as Dutchy quickly cut open a flap in the front of Scotty's wetsuit, running the scissors down from one armpit, then across the chest and down the other side. He peeled back the front of the wetsuit and Poppy immediately resumed compressions. She was aware of Ryder preparing the defibrillator but she had no time to watch him. She trusted him to do his job as he would have to trust her to do hers.

Ryder knelt opposite her. He had a towel in his hand and wiped it over Scotty's chest, drying it off before attaching the sticky pads for the defibrillator. His presence was reassuring. He worked calmly and quickly. He knew what he was doing. Like all the life-guards, he was well trained in the routine of pre-hospital care.

The defib charged and Poppy sat back, following the instructions from the mechanical voice. They all waited while the machine analysed the heart rhythm and then directed Ryder to apply a shock.

Scotty lifted off the ground as the machine delivered a charge, trying to shock his heart out of fibrillation and restore its normal rhythm.

They waited but there was no change.

'Continue CPR,' the machine instructed.

'Do you want me to swap places with you?' Ryder asked.

She lifted her head and looked into his eyes. She shook her head. 'I'm okay for another couple of rounds.' She was used to performing CPR. She resumed compressions while Dutchy fitted a face mask over Scotty's nose and mouth. A silicone bulb was attached to the mask, Dutchy would be able to take over from Scotty's brother and squeeze air into Scotty's lungs.

'Analysing rhythm.'

The defibrillator instructed them to stand clear.

'Delivering shock.'

Another jolt. But still no change. Poppy continued with a fifth round of compressions.

'The colour in his face is getting better,' Daisy said.

Poppy agreed. Even in the grey and overcast afternoon light she thought she could see some colour returning.

'Analysing rhythm.'

The defibrillator deliberated a possible third shock.

The verdict came back.

'No shock advised. Check pulse.'

Poppy completed her compressions while Ryder checked for a pulse. 'I've got something!'

Dutchy still held the mask over Scotty's face but before he could give any more rescue breaths Scotty lifted a hand and pushed Dutchy away.

'We've got him!'

Poppy couldn't believe it as Scotty coughed and his eyelids fluttered.

Daisy had the oxygen mask ready. Dutchy swapped the face mask for the smaller oxygen mask and looped the elastic behind Scotty's head.

'Come up here, where he can see you,' Poppy directed his brother, who was kneeling down by Scotty's feet. She knew Scotty would be disoriented and thought he'd respond better if he could see a familiar face amongst the crowd of strangers.

She spoke quietly to Scotty as his brother moved into view. 'You're on Bondi Beach. You were struck by lightning. We resuscitated you and now we're going to take you to hospital.'

Poppy, Ryder, Dutchy and Daisy rolled Scotty onto the stretcher and with Scotty's brother's help lifted him onto the back of the lifeguard buggy. Poppy sat with Scotty as Ryder and Dutchy quickly threw their bags into the buggy. Ryder climbed in the back next to Poppy and helped her stabilise the stretcher as Dutchy drove them all back to the tower.

Adrenalin coursed through her. Was it due to the incident that had just taken place or because Ryder was sitting beside her? She wasn't sure.

Her paramedic's uniform gave her confidence but even without it she knew she'd done a good job and thanks to all their efforts, and the defibrillator, it was a good outcome for Scotty, but she still felt shaky and she suspected it was because of Ryder's proximity.

She wanted to lean against him, lean on him, but she couldn't do it.

The ambulance was parked on the promenade, lights flashing, by the time they reached the steps to the tower.

Ryder reached for her hand to help her down from the buggy so they could offload Scotty. Even though she didn't really need his assistance, her body ached to touch him so she took the hand he offered her. His grip was gentle and warm and Poppy didn't want to let go but they needed to look after Scotty.

Alex was on duty and he came down the stairs and met them on the sand. Poppy briefed him while they transferred Scotty over, carrying him up to the promenade and loading him into the ambulance while his brother watched, still clearly dazed.

Poppy put her hand on his shoulder. 'Go with him,' she said.

Ryder added, 'We'll collect your boards and you can pick them up from here tomorrow.'

Poppy and Daisy were both shivering as the ambulance departed.

'You need to get warmed up,' Ryder said.

'I'll take the buggy and pick up the boards while I bring the flags and signs in,' Dutchy offered. The light was fading fast now and the beach had emptied of swimmers and people who had stayed to watch the drama unfolding, leaving just the lifeguards, Poppy and Daisy.

'Come on,' Ryder said as he opened the door to the tower. 'I'll put the kettle on. Are you okay?'

Poppy and Daisy both nodded. Neither of them were strangers when it came to emergencies, but a cup of tea was still welcome.

'Do you need to use the phone?' he asked Poppy as he filled the kettle.

'What for?'

'I thought you might want to let Craig know where you are. That you've been held up.'

Poppy shook her head. 'He didn't come down to Sydney in the end.' She had wondered whether or not she should tell Ryder that her plans had changed but had decided not to. Now she couldn't remember why she'd come to that decision. Had she thought going out to dinner with him might have been tempting fate? 'He got held up at work,' she explained.

'That's too bad,' he said without any trace of regret in his voice. 'Have you got plans for dinner? I could take you both out—as a thank you for doing my job for me?'

'I'm going out with friends from the hospital,' Daisy told him.

'I don't have plans,' Poppy said. Craig's cancellation had left her at a loose end.

Ryder grinned. 'How does Chinese and a couple of beers sound?' He paused, his brow furrowed as he asked, 'Do you drink beer?'

'I do.'

It was odd. She felt like she knew him so well still but the reality was that, after twelve years, they were strangers. But it didn't feel that way.

CHAPTER FOUR

Poppy washed and dried her hair, letting it curl naturally over her shoulders. She had agonised over what to wear and in the end settled on black jeans, a black shirt and a scarf with a geometric print with traces of green. She knew the green highlighted the colour of her eyes and she hadn't been able to resist adding it in a slight touch of vanity, even though she knew she wasn't going on a date. She was simply having dinner with an old friend.

But old friends didn't normally make her feel giddy and excited.

She wasn't convinced it was a good idea to have dinner for two, not considering the way he still made her feel, but she wasn't going to cancel. She knew she shouldn't be so eager given she was irritated with Craig, but she knew her feelings for Ryder were bordering on dangerous. But maybe she was looking at Ryder through rose-coloured glasses. Perhaps catching up with him over dinner would give her a chance to make some new memories, let go of her embarrassment from years gone by and settle her nerves, she thought as she drove back to the Bondi lifeguard tower to meet him.

He'd showered and changed and was also casually dressed in jeans and a T-shirt. That was good, he wasn't dressed for a date, but unfortunately the T-shirt sculpted his chest and arms and showed off his new muscles. That wasn't helpful.

Now that their emergency was over she had time to look at him more closely and she couldn't resist.

His thick hair was still slightly damp and his square jaw was darkened by a five o'clock shadow. The muscles and the stubble were new. He had matured. He was a man now, no longer a boy. Definitely not a boy and she was very aware of him.

'If you don't mind where we eat, I thought I'd try an Asian restaurant that Dutchy recommended in Bondi Junction.'

He jumped into her car and directed her to the restaurant. Her car wasn't small but it suddenly felt that way. The thunderstorm had passed but she could still feel electricity humming in the air and she knew it was her reaction to Ryder. He looked good and smelt even better.

She forced herself to focus on her driving and pulled into a park. Once she got out of the car her head cleared a little. A bit of distance eased her tension. She couldn't think straight when he was sitting so close.

The restaurant, Lao Lao's Kitchen, was small and busy and the scent of garlic and chilli competed with Ryder's scent. The tables were tightly packed but they found a small, empty one against a wall.

A young girl greeted them as she brought the menu. Her dark hair was tied in two pigtails that stuck out from the side of her head and she was missing two front teeth. She was very cute and Poppy guessed her to be about seven or eight years old. She must be the daughter of the owners.

'My grandpa will come and take your order,' she said as she put the menus on the table.

Poppy revised her assessment. Granddaughter of the owners probably.

'Thank you,' Poppy said to the girl as she poured water into their glasses.

She smiled at Poppy and Poppy felt a jolt of familiarity. As if she'd met the girl before.

'What is your name?' Poppy asked before the girl could leave, even though she couldn't possibly know her.

'An Na.'

Ryder pulled his chair into the table as the girl walked away. His knees banged into Poppy's, sending a bolt of electricity through her and stirring up the familiar feelings of desire once more.

She kept her eyes down, studying the menu as if her life depended on it. She couldn't look at him, he'd always been able to tell what she was thinking and she did not want him to read her mind right now.

She found herself unusually tongue-tied. She was normally quite opinionated and vocal, perhaps it had been a mistake coming to dinner *à deux*. She should have given more consideration to how he made her feel. She'd been telling herself they could rekindle their friendship but when she sat opposite him, close enough to see the different shades of blue in his eyes, close enough to feel his breath of the back of her hands, she couldn't deny that she was still attracted to him.

The attraction hadn't diminished after all those years and she found it disconcerting. Acknowledging her feelings, even silently, made her feel vulnerable, which added to her sense of unease.

But feeling attracted to Ryder was okay, she reassured herself as an elderly gentleman came to take their order. She didn't have to talk about it and she definitely didn't intend to act on it.

'Do you know what you'd like?' their waiter asked.

The menu had been a blur before her eyes, she'd been looking at it but hadn't been able to focus or concentrate. 'I'm happy with anything,' she said.

'Chef's choice?' Ryder asked.

'Sure.'

'Why don't you bring us a few of the chef's favourites?' Ryder requested. 'Maybe three small and a couple of larger dishes for us to share, and two beers. Thanks.'

'So, catch me up on the last twelve years,' he said as the waiter left the two of them alone.

Poppy laughed. 'That will take all night.'

'Sounds like you've got a lot to tell me.' He was smiling. 'Luckily I have plenty of time. There's nowhere else I need to be.'

He sat back in his chair and looked at her like he'd looked at her on the day she'd kissed him and she knew for certain that there was nowhere else she *wanted* to be.

'It feels strange,' she said.

'What does? Being here with me?'

'No.' That felt surprisingly good. Normal. Like old times. And that was what was so strange. That she should so easily slip back into their relationship. His company was easy. She knew that wasn't how he'd got his nickname, which came from a movie, but it suited his personality perfectly. At least in her opinion. 'I feel like it's only been weeks, months since I've seen you but it's really been almost half my life, yet I feel like you should still know everything that's happened.'

'So tell me. Get me up to speed and it will seem like the old days,' he said, and, once again his words accurately reflected her thoughts. 'You left Byron as soon as you finished school and headed to Brisbane?'

Poppy nodded.

'And became a paramedic? I thought medicine was high on your list, like Lily?'

'I realised I wasn't cut out for years of studying and ultimately I didn't want to be cooped up in a hospital or clinic. I wanted to help people but I also wanted to be amongst the action. Paramedic seemed a better fit. No two days are the same.'

She'd also worked out that she would be able to hide behind the uniform. She wouldn't need to form relationships with patients. Most of them she would only deal with once. That suited her perfectly. She wouldn't get attached to them and they wouldn't become too familiar, dependent or attached to her either. She wasn't good at close relationships, she preferred to keep her distance, and being a paramedic allowed her to do that.

'Have you been in Brisbane ever since?'

She shook her head. 'No. After I graduated from uni I worked in Brisbane for a couple of years and then I went to London. There were good jobs there for paramedics and I thought I wanted adventure.'

'You thought you did?'

She smiled. 'Turns out when I left Byron I was looking for a change, not adventure. When I moved to Brisbane it gave me a chance to find out who I was. You know what it was like in the commune,' she said. Ryder had spent countless hours with Poppy and Jet in the surf and at the commune and Poppy knew he would remember the dynamics.

'Us kids were seen and treated as one entity, by everyone really, the members of the commune and the public. If I wasn't seen as one of the commune kids I was seen as just another one of the Carlson tribe. I needed to find my own identity. Once I graduated and got some experience I wanted to push myself a bit more, test myself a bit more, so I went to London. It was fun for a while, for a summer, but I missed the sky and the sun and the weather and my siblings. I wanted a place to call home. I needed a place to call home and London wasn't it. So I came back.'

Her goal as a teenager had been to escape the commune as quickly as possible and it had taken her a while to figure out that the change she'd been looking for was security and stability, not adventure.

'And you met Craig in Brisbane?'

Poppy shook her head. 'We met in the UK. I travelled to the other side of the world and ended up meeting someone from Brisbane. I was really homesick; he was coming home and I decided to come back with him. It felt like it was meant to be.'

'It's serious with him? You're happy?'

Poppy hesitated. 'I think so.' It wasn't about being happy with Craig but how did she explain that without making herself sound weird. In her mind she was responsible for her own happiness. Her relationship with Craig was about achieving other goals. Her twin goals of security and stability.

'That doesn't sound very convincing. What's wrong? Are you unhappy in Sydney? Are you missing Craig?'

'Not really.' She had been finding herself more annoyed with him over the past couple of weeks. She didn't feel like she was a priority for him and considering everything she was giving up to make this move she found herself irritated. 'I just need a bit of time to adjust to the move.'

'It wasn't your idea?'

'No. Craig got promoted at work and the promotion meant a move to Sydney.'

'So you're following someone else's plan? That doesn't sound like you.'

He was right. She'd always set goals and timelines for herself and there had always been something she'd been working towards. Her current plan was to own her house. She imagined that having a place to call her own would provide her with the security and stability she needed and she was on her way to achieving her goal—admittedly with Craig's help—but now she'd let Craig change her plans and uproot her from her house. Was that why she was feeling unsettled? Because she was following Craig's plan? She was here in Sydney and where was he? Still in Brisbane.

Her plans had been derailed by Craig and somehow Ryder had spotted the problem.

'You didn't want to move here?' Ryder asked when Poppy hadn't verbalised her thoughts.

'I was happy to move…' She'd been happy to make the move to Sydney because it meant she and Craig could maintain the status quo of their relationship. Moving together meant they hadn't needed to have a conversation about their relationship and where it was headed, and Poppy was always happy to avoid conversations that focussed on her feelings. It had been far easier to agree to the move except now she was here and he wasn't. If it hadn't been for her siblings—and Ryder, added the little voice in her head—she would be even more annoyed.

'But?'

'But the plan was that we move together but now I'm here and he's still in my house in Brisbane.'

'You have a house there?'

'Well, we do. Craig and I bought it together. I miss my house,' she admitted, choosing not to outline that she missed the house more than she missed Craig. She and Craig hadn't discussed how long the move to Sydney would be for but Poppy knew she had never imagined leaving her home permanently.

'You miss your house!' The surprise was evident in Ryder's voice. 'It's just a building.'

She shook her head. 'It's more than that. It's my sanctuary. Growing up in the commune, we never had any privacy and then I lived in a university college and that was the same. I want somewhere that is mine, somewhere that reflects me.' She knew that Ryder was one of the few people she knew, one of the *only* people she knew, who would understand her logic.

'And does it reflect you?'

'It needs a lot of work.' She laughed. 'It needs time and love and money. It might reflect me more than I realised.'

'So you're going to keep it? You're not planning on selling it?'

'No!' She had spent endless hours working on their house and working additional shifts to pay for it. The house was a labour of love and she hadn't contemplated selling it. She *wouldn't* contemplate that. 'I have put my heart and soul into that house. I'll get the renovations finished and then we'll have to rent it out but I'm not going to sell it.' She knew that wasn't the agreement she and Craig had made but she still hoped to be able to change his mind.

'And Craig. Does he love it as much as you do?'

'He's not as attached to it as I am,' she admitted. 'He sees it as a good investment. He's an accountant,' she added by way of explanation.

'I'm sure you'll be able to convince him to keep it if it means that much to you.'

She wasn't so certain.

'A man in love will do anything,' Ryder added.

'I don't think that's the case.'

'Really? It is in my experience.'

Poppy hadn't been disagreeing with Ryder's opinion but rather with the idea that Craig loved her. 'Have you been in love?' she asked.

He nodded. 'Twice.'

'Twice!' She wondered about the type of women Ryder had loved. What did he look for?

'What about you?'

'Once,' she said. 'And I got my heart broken. I don't want to feel like that again.' She had never forgotten the pain of her first heartbreak. Losing Ryder had had long-lasting repercussions on her impressionable teenage heart.

'So you're not in love now? You're not in love with Craig?'

'We're compatible.'

'That's not what I asked.'

'We have similar goals.'

'That doesn't sound very romantic.'

'Romance isn't a high priority.' She still wasn't sure what she expected from a relationship but she knew she wasn't in love with Craig. And she didn't want to be. Love was fickle. Love led to heartbreak.

'But it should be,' he said. 'You should be spoiled, adored, loved. Life is too short to miss out on all those things.'

Coming from Ryder's lips, those words sounded wonderful but Poppy couldn't imagine they applied to her. In her world love wasn't reciprocated. She'd never felt adored by her parents and Ryder had left before she'd ever had a chance to find out what might happen. And surely their teenage love wouldn't have lasted.

She was unlovable and it was better not to expect too much. It was better not to dream of love.

'Tell me. How does Craig make you feel?'

Ryder always used to ask how she was feeling. Was she okay? Was she happy? Was she sad? Craig never asked. And she didn't want him to. She didn't want to discuss her feelings.

She didn't want to feel.

She didn't want to hurt.

'Does he make you feel like you can't live without him?' Ryder asked her. 'Does he make you feel excited? Like the world is a better place, a brighter, more positive place?'

'Is that how love feels?'

He had just described exactly how she had felt as a teenager.

He nodded. 'You remember what it was like,' he said.

Was he reading her mind again? 'What *what* was like?' she asked, even though she was afraid of what his answer would be.

'How it felt to be seventeen. Or, in your case, sixteen.'

Poppy swallowed. She remembered every minute detail. How Ryder had tasted. How he'd felt. How her breath had caught in her throat. How her pulse had raced. How her heart had broken.

He held her captive with his gaze as he said, 'You remember that sense of excitement, of anticipation. Like nothing else in the world mattered. That first amazing teenage kiss.'

Poppy nodded. She remembered that kiss like it was yesterday. 'I thought you'd forgotten all about that. It was so long ago.'

'No,' he said, shaking his head. 'I've never forgotten. That was the best and worst day of my young life. Finding out we were leaving Byron Bay and then getting kissed by you. Mind you, the best and worst wasn't in that order,' he said with a smile.

'And then I never heard from you again,' she accused.

'I know. I'm sorry, I had no idea what to say.'

'I thought about coming to find you,' Poppy said. She'd been upset when he'd left but also envious that he'd managed to escape. She couldn't wait to get out of Byron. She'd thought she was destined for bigger and better things but, in hindsight, it hadn't been all bad. But once Ryder had left her life had felt drained of colour and she had fantasised about running away to be with him. By the end of the following year, when she'd finished high school and had been accepted into university in Brisbane, she had put him to the back of her mind.

'Why didn't you?'

She shrugged. 'It was just a teenage fantasy. I felt that you understood me in a way no one else did, especially my parents, and when you left I felt like I'd lost someone really important, but running away wasn't very realistic. I knew I had to finish school.'

'You stuck to your plan.'

'I guess I did. When I didn't hear from you, I realised how foolish the idea of running away was and getting an education and using that to get out of Byron seemed a bit more sensible. I guess I grew up.' And forgot about falling in love. She had seen from Lily's example that studying hard was the way to get out of Byron.

Despite the fact that she was being forced to remember those foolish teenage days and emotions, she was enjoying Ryder's company. Even if she didn't want to talk about her feelings he was happy to listen to her talk about her plans. He always had been and she had lapped up his attention. He had made her feel that her ideas were worth something. That they were important. That *she* was important.

'Have you been back to Byron recently?' Ryder asked. 'How are your mum and dad?'

'They're well, I guess.'

'You guess? You haven't seen them?'

'Not for a while,' she admitted. Some people might argue that a year was longer than 'a while' but Poppy was never in a hurry to return to Byron Bay. She accepted it was a beautiful place but she was quite happy to leave it to the hordes of tourists who flocked to the district.

'You must have driven through Byron on your way here. You didn't stop?'

'It wasn't the right spot to stop. I wanted to get closer to Sydney before I broke the journey.' Byron was only a two-hour drive from Brisbane on the direct route to Sydney but she'd deliberately driven for an extra hour before stretching her legs. 'They wouldn't have cared if I stopped or not. You know we're not close.' She shrugged. That was why she'd kept on driving. The reception she would have received would not have been the one she'd hoped for and so she'd decided it was better to keep driving and avoid the disappointment.

She knew she should get over herself. Plenty of people had grown up in worse environments than she had and she was fortunate to have her siblings, but it didn't change the fact that she had never felt valued or loved by her own parents.

Growing up in the commune, parenting had been a collective responsibility. Her father, Pete, had spent time with them in the surf but that had usually been a group activity with numerous children, not just the Carlson siblings. There had been very little time spent alone as a family unit. There had always been other people around and Poppy didn't feel she'd ever formed a close bond with either of her parents.

Neither of them were demonstrative or overly affectionate, her mother in particular, and Poppy often wondered if she had even wanted kids. She knew Goldie had fallen pregnant unexpectedly with Lily when she'd only been nineteen but she'd gone on to have four more children. Surely they hadn't all been mistakes?

'They're still your parents,' Ryder interrupted her thoughts.

'Don't judge me,' she said. Ryder might be a good listener but she did *not* want to talk about her parents. 'Why don't we talk about your family for a bit? They're not nearly as crazy as mine.'

'Maybe not as extraordinary as yours but we've had our fair share of drama and dysfunction, although thankfully we seem to be coming out the other side now.'

Poppy couldn't imagine Ryder creating drama. He'd always been her stabilising influence. Sure, he'd joined in on their wild, youthful escapades but he was far from dysfunctional. From her perspective he'd had a perfectly normal family.

'What drama did you have?'

'Aside from my dad's affair with a colleague, you mean?'

'Aside from that.' People had affairs all the time and while she disagreed with it in principle it was hardly unusual and, in her mind, it didn't make his family any more dysfunctional than many others. Particularly when compared to hers.

Ryder hadn't spoken to his father in years. His dad's affair had been the reason his mother had dragged him and his sister across the country to Perth. Ryder's parents had been teachers and they'd taught at the same school. Their marriage had broken down when his father had had an affair with another teacher and his mother had taken the children and left. Ryder blamed his father not only for breaking his mother's heart but for having the affair that had forced their move to Western Australia. The move that had ripped him away from Poppy.

'We lived with my grandmother when we first got to Perth, Mum's mum, but that didn't go so well. Mum was pretty fragile and I think she was hoping for some emotional support but my grandmother was more in favour of the "put on a brave face and get on with things" approach. Mum just seemed to give up. She spent a lot of time in her room, which didn't help Lucy. Lucy was only young and she needed her mother. Things were a bit of a mess for a while.'

That was an understatement but he didn't want to go into specifics tonight. It wasn't a cheerful subject. His mother had started drinking and his sister had stopped eating. It had been a cry for help but he hadn't recognised it at the time and he had blamed himself for some of his sister's suffering. For a long time he'd felt there was more he could have, should have, done. He'd felt like he failed both his mother and his sister. He'd tried to give them what they'd needed but he hadn't been able to. What they'd needed most had been his father and he'd let them all down.

'They're both doing better now,' he said. 'Mum has a new partner, he's a nice guy, and Lucy has turned the corner. That's why I could embark on my road trip.'

Steve was a good addition to their family and knowing his mum and his sister had someone to watch over them helped Ryder sleep at night.

'Are you running away from home?' Poppy teased.

'No.' A part of him wished he could stay in Bondi but that hadn't been his plan and he knew he was only thinking of it now because of Poppy. But it wasn't really on his agenda. 'I'll be going back. They still need me.'

'And what about what you need?' she asked. 'What about your hopes and dreams and plans? What do you want?'

He wanted Poppy.

Seeing her again had made him realise that he'd never truly got over her. It was crazy to think those old feelings were still there, as all-consuming as ever. He wondered if he should tell her but decided against it. What was the point? It was likely to make one of them feel uncomfortable and it was irrelevant now any-way—as long as she was in a relationship, she was off limits.

He wished he could be happy for her but in his opinion it didn't sound as though she had found the perfect guy. She should have romance and love. She might want security—who didn't?—but he suspected she still had more of her parents' free spirit in her than she cared to admit. And she needed to be given a chance to soar. He didn't think she should be constrained by finances and budgets. She had always had plans but that had been to escape Byron Bay. He'd thought she'd travel, see the world. Perhaps her idea of escape was different from his.

Despite that, he could understand her desire for a home to call her own. The commune had been chaotic but he had loved it. It had been a happy environment, although he could see how it might have been overwhelming if it was your home, but he'd never pictured her choosing to live in a city. He'd thought she'd feel stifled. She needed freedom. The surf. The sun. She was bound to the earth and the ocean and the sky.

But twelve years was a long time and the Poppy he'd known had changed. She'd grown up, taken on responsibility. He could understand her need for stability but he wondered whether the old Poppy was still in there somewhere. The one who'd run wild in the bush and surfed off the rocks.

He hoped so.

Ryder watched the ocean, double-checking every woman with blonde hair, wondering if he would see Poppy. He had tried to forget her, he had tried not to compare all other women to her, but after dinner last night he was finding it impossible not to think about her. Their connection had been special and he felt it still. It wasn't just because of shared history, it went deeper than that, yet he couldn't explain why he should feel this connection with her and only her. He didn't believe in soul mates. At least, not until he was around her.

His kept his mind on Poppy but his eyes on the sea. The ocean was calm for the moment but the day was warm and he knew people had a tendency to get complacent when the water was flat. It wasn't as threatening but the water was just as deep and the tides could still take you out of your depth or wash you off a sand bar. You could drown just as easily on a calm day if you weren't a confident swimmer.

Ryder felt like the ocean. One minute he'd been calm, rolling towards a life in Perth and a new career, when suddenly the wind had blown in and brought change. Seeing Poppy again made him rethink his vague plans. He was flexible and returning to Perth was optional. He could go wherever his career, his life or love took him.

What if Poppy was still his perfect woman? Twelve years ago he'd thought that she was the one but teenage hormones didn't translate into everlasting love—did they?

He needed to find out who she had become. It sounded like she was focussed, she still had her goals set. That was the Poppy he'd known—full of plans. But her plans now were about security and stability. Her plans were all financial. What had happened to the Poppy who'd been eager to escape Byron Bay? What had happened to the Poppy who had planned to conquer the world? Who'd had such a zest for life? For living? What did she dream about? Was she happy?

Was Craig the love of her life?

It didn't sound like that to Ryder but what did he know? He'd been spectacularly unlucky in love.

Maybe Craig was exactly what Poppy wanted. What she needed.

She'd bought a house with Craig—that was a serious step, more serious than just living together in a rental. It smacked of something more permanent. She hadn't exactly been singing his praises but perhaps she'd just been trying to spare Ryder's feelings?

She wanted security and stability and Craig was giving her that.

Ryder knew he couldn't compete. Not at the moment. How was a mature age student, waiting to get his career started and who worked as a casual lifeguard with nothing to his name, going to be able to provide her with the things she wanted?

But what if Poppy was supposed to be with him? What if she was the one? Still the one.

But he was jumping ahead of himself. Way ahead. Indulging in his fantasies. He still had a memory in his head left over from twelve years ago about what life with Poppy would look like. But there was nothing to say he would get that chance.

He hoped he wouldn't have to be content with friendship, he thought as his attention was captured by the sight of a bikini-clad girl running up to the buggy.

'There's a man down the beach,' she said as she waved her arm towards the north end of the beach, 'having some sort of fit.'

'Jump in,' Ryder said, pushing his own thoughts aside. 'Can you take me to him?'

The girl nodded and climbed into the ATV, stepping over the rescue board that was stored on the passenger side of the buggy.

Ryder started the engine and headed north, driving along the wet, hard-packed sand. He picked up the radio as he drove and called the incident into the tower. 'Central, this is Easy. I've got a report of a man having a seizure on the beach. I'm checking it out and will update you.'

'Copy that. I'll send Bluey to assist.'

Ryder hit the siren on the buggy, clearing the crowds as he weaved his way up the beach.

'Over there.' The girl pointed to her left.

Ryder could see a large crowd gathering on the sand. He hit the kill switch on the ATV as he brought it to a stop several metres from the crowd. He knew he wasn't going to be able to drive any closer. He jumped out and grabbed the two-way radio and the medical kit and ran through the soft sand, pushing his way through the onlookers.

As the crowd parted Ryder saw an elderly gentleman lying on a towel in full sun. He was convulsing, his eyes were rolled back in his head and he was frothing at the mouth. Ryder crouched down beside him. 'Sir, I'm a lifeguard. I'm here to help you.'

As he'd expected, there was no response.

He looked up at the crowd. 'Is there anyone here who knows this man?'

No one spoke up and then the girl who'd fetched him said, 'He seemed to be by himself. My friends and I were sitting nearby. There didn't seem to be anyone with him.'

'No one who has gone swimming perhaps?' Ryder asked. But there was only one towel, which the man was lying on, and no bags or any evidence that someone else had been there.

The girls shook her head.

Ryder called the tower again. 'Central, I'm going to need some help and an ambulance. I have an unidentified elderly male having a seizure. Unknown onset. Non-responsive but breathing.'

Jet's reply came back. 'Bluey is on his way. I'll call the ambos.'

There wasn't much Ryder could do. The man was possibly dehydrated but he had no way of getting fluids into him. He was lying in full sun and getting him into the shade was probably the best he could manage until help arrived. He looked around. There were dozens of beach umbrellas stuck into the sand.

'Could someone hold an umbrella over us for some shade?' he asked as he heard Bluey pushing his way through the mass of people that seemed to be growing by the second. As usual, a drama attracted spectators.

The seizure abated as Bluey arrived, carrying the oxygen and the defib unit.

The man had stopped thrashing and foaming at the mouth but his eyes were still glazed and Ryder could tell he wasn't aware of his surroundings. Far from it.

Ryder had no way of telling what had caused the seizure. Epilepsy would be his guess but it could be any number of things and whatever the cause the seizure had lasted several minutes making it a medical emergency.

He was able to take the man's pulse, his heart was racing, but when he tried to hook the oxygen mask over the man's mouth and nose the man lashed out, knocking the mask from Ryder's hands.

'Sir? Can you hear me? You're on Bondi Beach, and you've a had a seizure, I'm a lifeguard and I want to give you some oxygen.' Ryder spoke quietly and clearly as he tried again to position the mask but the man had the same reaction. He wondered what the man thought was happening.

He picked up the radio and called Jet. 'How far away are the ambos?' he asked. He needed their help. There was no way he and Bluey could get this patient onto a stretcher and back to the tower without assistance.

'Gibbo's bringing them over in a buggy. They're almost with you.'

The crowd parted as Jet finished speaking and Ryder could see Poppy coming towards him just as he managed to secure the oxygen mask in place. He breathed out a sigh of relief.

Poppy knelt in the sand beside him. 'Hey, what have we got?'

Ryder told her what he knew, which was

very little. 'Elderly gentleman having a seizure that lasted several minutes. It took me a few minutes to reach him and the fit continued for more than five after I arrived on the scene. He was breathing but was non-responsive. He's still non-responsive and agitated. Nil communication. Pulse ninety-six. No companions. No ID. No Medic Alert.'

Poppy was nodding. 'Was his whole body seizing or just his limbs?'

'His whole body. And quite violently. We've put the umbrella over him now but he was in full sun.'

'Does he have a bag with him?' Poppy asked. 'Any medication?'

'I haven't seen a bag. There was an empty water bottle beside him and the towel he's lying on, that seems to be it.' The man's eyes were closed now but Ryder could hear him breathing in the oxygen.

Poppy's colleague squatted beside them and spoke to the man. 'Sir, we're from the ambulance.' Alex put his hand on the man's shoulder but the man reacted violently again, just as he'd done with Ryder, but this time his fist connected with Alex, startling everyone.

The man's eyes opened as Alex kept talking. Clearly distressed, he continued to hit out, pushing Alex away. He pulled the oxygen mask from his face but still didn't speak. He pointed to his ears.

Ryder watched as Poppy nodded and said, 'It's okay, I understand.' She was signing as she spoke.

She turned around and looked at Ryder. 'He's deaf,' she explained.

CHAPTER FIVE

POPPY SAW RYDER'S expression clear as her words went some way to explain the man's reaction. She turned back to the patient. He had calmed down slightly but still looked frightened. She knew that patients coming out of a fit were often disoriented and scared and she imagined it must be doubly frightening for someone who was deaf or had an additional disability. Her hands flew as she explained what had happened.

I'm a paramedic, she signed as she touched the symbol on her uniform. *You are on Bondi Beach. You had a seizure. Do you understand?*

She spoke quietly, her words accompanying her hands, letting him choose to either read her lips or her hands. Slowly, he calmed down.

I'm going to put the oxygen mask back on for you. Is that okay?

Poppy kept her information as brief as possible, knowing it would be easier for him if he could give her yes or no answers.

What is your name?

Anthony, he signed.

My name is Poppy. Have you had a fit before, Anthony?

He nodded his head.

My colleague and I are just going to check your condition. Is that okay?

She waited for him to nod before asking Alex to start taking his obs and speaking to the lifeguards. 'I'm just explaining to him what happened,' she said, as Alex slipped a pulse oximeter onto his finger. 'He's an epileptic. His name is Anthony.'

Anthony was signing to her.

That's okay, we understand, she signed back.

'He's apologising for striking out. He was confused when he woke up and with so many people surrounding him he thought he was being attacked,' she told the others as she wrapped the blood-pressure cuff around Anthony's arm.

She turned back to the patient. *Is there anyone with you? Family? A friend?*

He shook his head, signed, *My wife is at work.*

Poppy nodded. *We need to take you to hospital. Okay?*

He shook his head, surprising her. She hadn't thought he would refuse. His condition had stabilised so it was no longer an emergency but he still needed to be properly assessed.

You need to be assessed. You're probably dehydrated. It's a hot day so you will probably need a drip. That might be all and then you will be able to go home. I can call your wife for you and get her to meet us at the hospital.

He nodded and signed, *Okay.*

Will she be able to hear me? Poppy knew that there were a lot of deaf couples in society. She needed to make sure Anthony's wife would be able to hear her.

Anthony nodded and Poppy pulled her phone from a pocket in the side of her trousers.

'I'm just going to call Anthony's wife to let her know what has happened and to get her to meet us at Bondi General. Can you load him on a stretcher, and we'll get him to the ambulance?'

Poppy unloaded the stretcher in the emergency bay at Bondi General. She had travelled in the back with Anthony and he was quite stable and seemed much calmer now. She'd called ahead and asked for Lily to meet them, knowing it would help Anthony to be assessed by a doctor who could also sign.

This is Dr Carlson, Poppy told him. *She will take care of you. She can sign too.*

Poppy saw him do a double take when he saw Lily.

She looks like you.

Poppy smiled. *She is my sister. You're in good hands. Your wife is on her way.*

Thank you.

My pleasure, she signed as they pushed the stretcher into the hospital before transferring him to a hospital barouche and leaving him with Lily.

'Was everything okay with Anthony?' Poppy asked as she stepped out onto the deck and handed Lily a glass of wine.

'Yes, poor man. He was pretty confused but he was okay. He had some IV fluids and then his wife took him home.'

Poppy's shift had been busy and halfway through she'd debated the wisdom of putting her hand up for the extra hours given that she'd got home late last night after dinner with Ryder, but Craig's no-show had left her with time on her hands and she was pleased she'd been there for Anthony. She'd hoped she'd helped him to negotiate what would have been a scary event. 'It would have been terrifying for him.'

'He was lucky that you were there, really.'

'I keep thinking what if that had been Daisy in that situation.' The idea made Poppy feel emotional. 'She'd be so vulnerable.'

'She doesn't have any underlying health problems.'

'I know, but if she was in an accident and alone, who would take care of her? Who's going to take care of any of us?'

Lily frowned and sipped her wine. 'What are you talking about?'

'Do you think there's something wrong with us? Do you think there's a reason we can't have successful relationships? Daisy's never had a serious boyfriend. Jet has had a million short-term flings and you and Otto aren't exactly living in marital bliss.'

'What about you and Craig? You're living together. That's a pretty serious relationship if you ask me.'

'I'm not living with him right now, I'm living with you. I put myself in the same category. We're all screwed up. I should be living with Craig and you should be living with Otto and yet, here we are, living here with Daisy like three spinsters.'

'I don't think it's as bad as all that.'

'Don't you?'

'No. You and Craig are only apart temporarily.'

Poppy knew that wasn't really at the core of her concerns. She and Craig didn't spend much time together anyway and she wasn't really missing him. And that was the problem. She wasn't missing Craig and she couldn't stop thinking about Ryder. If she and Craig were going to make it as a couple, should she be spending so much time thinking about another man?

'And what about you and Otto?' she asked, in an effort to get her mind off Ryder. 'What is happening with the two of you?'

Lily sighed. 'I don't know.'

'Do you miss him?'

'I try not to think about it.'

Poppy fell silent as she thought about Lily and Otto. In her opinion they were perfect together and if they weren't going to make it Poppy knew she would lose all faith in any of the Carlson siblings being able to sustain a serious relationship.

'What's bothering you? This isn't just about me and Otto, is it?' Lily asked. She always knew when something was troubling her siblings. It was part of her role in the family, to fix things.

Poppy wished she could fix things for Lily but she knew it wasn't that easy. For a start, Lily would have to *want* to fix things.

'I'm just thinking about missed opportunities,' she said.

In the few quiet moments she'd had during her shift today she'd found herself constantly reliving last night's dinner. Recalling how easily the conversation had flowed, how they had laughed and finished each other's sentences. How the twelve years apart had dissolved in the space of a few hours and how they had quickly re-established their easy camaraderie.

Dinner with Ryder had also made her examine her relationship with Craig.

She knew she was with Craig because he was a safe choice. They might not have amazing chemistry but she had convinced herself she didn't want that. She didn't want to feel out of control. She didn't want to feel vulnerable.

Her parents, her mother in particular, were not affectionate, not demonstrative with their feelings, and Poppy had never felt unconditionally loved by either of them. And then Ryder, her first love, had left her. She'd learned from experience that love was a painful emotion. It was better to learn to live without it. Wanting something you couldn't have was only going to lead to heartache.

She didn't want to look for love. She didn't want to risk rejection.

Or so she'd been telling herself.

She knew Craig wasn't going to break her heart but why then did she get the feeling she'd made a mistake? The buzz she got from being with Ryder—was it a mistake to never feel that with anyone else? Was she so afraid of rejection that she was willing to live in the shadows?

Being with Ryder made her feel as if she was in full sunshine, her world was right, happy. She was able to live in the moment. Ryder reminded her of the girl she used to be. The girl who had laughed and dreamed. Where had that girl gone?

She'd lost her sense of adventure. She'd replaced it with a good work ethic but were the two mutually exclusive?

She'd had a goal to own her own house and she hadn't achieved it yet but it wasn't far off—half a house with Craig still counted—and maybe once she'd ticked that box she could think about what she wanted next.

'Did something happen with Craig?'

'No.' Poppy shook her head as she topped up their wine glasses. 'With Ryder.'

'Ryder?'

Poppy nodded. 'I kissed him.'

'What!' Lily almost choked on a mouthful of wine. 'When? Last night?' Lily knew that Poppy and Ryder had caught up for dinner.

'No, not last night. Twelve years ago.'

'Oh.' Poppy heard the relief in Lily's voice and she knew her sister thought it was all water under the bridge and nothing to worry about. What she didn't know was that Poppy wanted to do it all over again. 'That was so long ago, why are you thinking about it now?'

'I can't *stop* thinking about it. I hadn't thought about him for years but since I've seen him again I can't get it out of my mind and it's making me wonder what I'm doing with Craig.' She didn't divulge that she wanted to kiss Ryder again. That information wasn't for sharing, not even with Lily. 'Isn't absence supposed to make the heart grow fonder?' Poppy asked, wondering if that was the case for Lily and Otto.

'Supposedly. That's not how you're feeling?'

'No.'

'Is Ryder your missed opportunity?'

'I think he might be,' Poppy admitted.

'And how does he fit into your plans?'

He didn't fit in with her plans. Not at all.

He stirred all sorts of emotions in her, simultaneously making her feel calm and nervous. Her soul was calm when she was with him, even if her heart was racing and her knees were shaky. When she was with Ryder she felt like she was where she was supposed to be, was who she was supposed to be, but she knew he didn't fit in with her plans.

But she couldn't bring herself to say that. Admitting that would mean he wouldn't be part of her life in the future and she wasn't ready to say goodbye to him again. Not yet.

She remained silent.

'I think you should go and see Craig,' Lily suggested. 'See how you feel after a weekend in Brisbane. Ryder is gorgeous and sort of familiar but perhaps seeing him is confusing your feelings for Craig.'

Poppy paid the cab driver and lifted her bag from the seat. She pushed open the front gate and saw Craig's car in the driveway. She hadn't told him she was coming. She'd had a feeling he'd try to talk her out of it and she knew she couldn't put it off.

She needed to get herself back on an even

keel. Lily had been right. Spending some time with Craig would help to remind her of why they were together. Coming home would give her a chance to put Ryder out of her mind. A chance to focus on Craig and on their relationship.

She stood inside the front gate and took a moment to assess her feelings. She was restless and had a strange sense of foreboding. Was it just because Ryder had unsettled her equilibrium or was it due to something else? She had no idea but surely she should be feeling differently? She was about to see Craig for the first time in three weeks. Shouldn't she be excited, eager, happy?

But she was none of those things.

She was pleased to be home but she felt like something was missing. Someone.

She shook her head. She was being ridiculous. It was time to grow up and time to put Ryder out of her mind.

She shut the gate and climbed the steps leading to the front of the house.

The bottom step was loose and the paint on the wooden banister flaked off under her hand. She added those two jobs to the long list she already had. She breathed in the scent of the frangipani that grew in the corner between the house and the staircase. She loved that perfume and if she closed her eyes she could picture how the house would look, the fragrant flowers of the frangipani with its glossy green leaves contrasting with the freshly painted white woodwork of the façade. One day her house would be perfect.

She pushed open the wooden louvre doors on the small veranda and slid her key into the front door. The house was in darkness save for a sliver of light that spilled into the passage from the master bedroom, where the door was slightly ajar. She was about to push the bedroom door open when she heard water running in the bathroom at the back of the house. Was Craig in the shower?

She paused, waiting to feel a sense of expectation and eagerness over seeing Craig again, but there was nothing. Their relationship wasn't built on sexual chemistry, it was built on shared goals and mutual respect and that had been enough for her. Until now, a little voice in her head said.

She hoped Lily was right. She hoped this visit would give her what she needed. An opportunity to remind herself of the value of their relationship. Of the benefits.

She dropped her bag and walked the length of the passage. She'd surprise Craig in the shower, she thought as she heard the water

shut off. Maybe she just needed to try harder
to breathe some life into their relationship,
she thought as she tried not to think about
how differently she'd feel if it was Ryder in
the shower.

The bathroom door swung open before
she could reach it. Poppy had expected to
see Craig emerge and she froze, momentarily
confused, when she saw a woman coming
towards her. Her first thought was they had
an intruder but as her brain caught up with
her eyes she realised the woman was almost
naked, wearing nothing but an unbuttoned
man's business shirt and a pair of bikini
briefs. Poppy didn't recognise the woman but
she recognised the shirt. It was one of Craig's.
One she'd bought him.

'Who the hell are you?'

The woman looked a little startled but not
as thrown by the situation as Poppy thought
she should be. She recovered quickly. 'Dee.'

That told Poppy nothing. And why was she
almost naked?

The picture gradually came into focus. It
was surely only seconds but it felt like an
eternity. Craig's car in the drive. A light on in
the bedroom—*her* bedroom—a semi-naked
woman coming out of the bathroom.

Craig was cheating on her.

She turned her back on the woman—Dee—and shoved the bedroom door open, taking some small delight in seeing the horrified expression on Craig's face when he saw her standing there instead of the woman he had been expecting.

She would have laughed at his expression except that she was furious and embarrassed. She hated being wrong-footed. She hated feeling like a fool.

She was the planner. The one who always knew how things would end. The one who had an end game. Or at least she had been until the last couple of weeks. Ryder had unsettled her life and now it looked as though Craig was adding to her confusion.

She hadn't told Craig she was coming so that he couldn't convince her not to. She'd wanted him be the one who was surprised. Turned out they were both surprised.

The trouble was, she hated surprises. She hated losing control.

'Poppy!' Craig was sitting on the edge of the bed, checking his phone. It didn't look so bad—if she ignored the fact that he was naked. 'I wasn't expecting you.'

'Evidently.'

She could feel Dee hovering behind her. She stretched her arm out, putting her hand on the doorframe, blocking her entry, shutting her out.

Craig grabbed a pillow and put it over his lap. Poppy wasn't sure why. She'd seen him naked plenty of times but he was obviously feeling uncomfortable. She hoped he was feeling guilty.

'Is there something you've forgotten to tell me?' She wasn't sure how she was managing to sound calm and rational. She'd caught Craig cheating on her so she should be throwing things, screaming at him or bursting into tears—all those things she'd seen in the movies—but although she felt like an idiot she was far from devastated.

If anything, it reinforced that she'd been sensible not to fall in love. If she'd loved Craig then his infidelity would hurt far more.

She felt foolish but not heartbroken.

She turned to Dee. 'I think you should leave.' Her voice was quiet but steely. She shot a glare in Dee's direction but knew she would save most of her anger for Craig. Just because she wasn't heartbroken it didn't mean he would escape without hearing her thoughts on his behaviour.

'I'll drive you home.'

Craig had pulled on a pair of shorts while she'd been glaring at Dee.

'No, you won't,' Poppy told him. She folded her arms. 'She can take your car or you can call her a cab but you are staying here. I think there are some things we need to discuss.' She wasn't sure where she got the courage to speak to him like that. The shock made her bolshy.

Was this what he'd been getting up to? Was this why he hadn't come down to Sydney as planned? Was this a one-off or something more? Was Dee the reason he'd been hard to get hold of? Was she what was keeping him busy—not work and not golf?

She hated feeling like a fool and she hated being made a fool of even more. Was he taking her for one?

No more.

'What's going on?' she asked once Dee had left and she and Craig had moved their discussion to the living room. She wasn't comfortable having this conversation in their bedroom given the circumstances and that annoyed her. 'Was this your way of telling me it's over? You wanted me to catch you being unfaithful?'

'No! I would never do that. I wasn't expecting you. You didn't tell me you were coming back. I didn't want to hurt you.'

She had to believe him. He was safe, dependable, reliable, and she didn't think he would deliberately hurt her. That was one of the things she liked about him.

'I want you to be happy,' he continued. 'I want us both to be happy and I know I'm not. I haven't been happy for a long time and I don't think you're happy either.'

Was he right?

She knew he was.

A month ago she would have argued that she was happy but now she knew that wasn't true. She just hadn't realised that something was missing from her life.

'You spend all your time either at work or working on the house,' Craig said. 'We don't do anything together and I don't want to spend my life like that. We're like flatmates. We don't talk about anything other than this house and your plans for it. I thought moving to Sydney might give us a different purpose, something else to focus on, but I've been happier since you left.'

Poppy felt cut to the bone. 'With Dee?'

He nodded. 'I really did intend to speak to you. Life has to be better than what we had. I want passion, excitement. I want more.'

He wasn't apologising. He didn't sound sorry. She supposed no one should apologise for being happy. Or for being right.

There was no excitement in their relationship but that was what she'd thought she wanted. Right up until the moment Ryder had reappeared in her life.

She knew she'd been lying to herself. She wanted excitement. She wanted desire. She wanted that buzz.

But she also wanted stability and security. Could she have it all?

Stability, security and excitement?

Maybe not. But perhaps this was her chance to find out.

Could she explore things with Ryder without giving up her goals? Without giving up everything?

She knew that was impossible. There would be some risk. Was she brave enough?

Poppy turned her phone on as she walked off the plane, ready to let Lily know she'd arrived, but as she walked through the gate lounge she heard a familiar, but unexpected, voice.

'Hey, how are you doing?'

'Ryder!' Poppy's smile was wide and spontaneous. She'd been feeling like a complete fool but the unexpected sight of Ryder was enough to immediately cheer her up.

'What are you doing here?'

'Lily got called into work,' he said as he

slung an arm around her shoulder as he walked beside her. Poppy almost missed a step as Ryder's touch triggered the now familiar buzz of excitement and anticipation to burst through her. It didn't escape her notice that this was the exact buzz that had been missing when she'd gone to see Craig. She'd tried to reason with herself as to why the buzz wasn't necessary but she knew she was kidding herself. The buzz was addictive and she wanted more. 'Jet and Daisy are working too,' he continued, 'so Lily asked me to collect you.'

Poppy wondered if that was true or if Lily was meddling. Her head was still spinning and she knew she didn't have the capacity to work out what was going on. Did Ryder know what had happened?'

'I could have taken a cab.'

'I wasn't sure if you'd want company. If you want to be alone I'll drop you home and take off.'

She was quiet throughout the car trip. Sorting through her thoughts. Wondering how much to tell Ryder. He had always been a good listener, a sounding board, and she supposed he would be no different now, but did she want to discuss the drama of her love life, the failings of her relationship with him? She wasn't sure.

She was still undecided when Ryder turned his car into Moore Street and pulled up in front of Lily's house.

'Thanks for the lift.'

'No worries. What are you going to do now?'

There was nothing she needed to do. She was home a day earlier than planned so her time was her own but she felt caged. Restless. 'I might go for a walk.' It was early evening, still light, and a walk might help her to relax.

'Would you like company?'

She nodded. 'I would.'

Ryder's company would be a good distraction. She was angry and upset but she didn't want to be alone with her thoughts. He might be able to keep her mind off her own short-comings.

She knew she didn't love Craig so being rejected by him shouldn't hurt but that wasn't the case. She'd thought her heart was tougher than this. It wasn't his infidelity that hurt her but his rejection of her. Once again, she'd been found to be undeserving of someone's love.

'Did Lily tell you what happened?' Poppy asked as they headed along the cliff top walk towards Tamarama Beach.

'Not exactly. She just said you'd had a

shock and were flying back early. I assumed it had something to do with Craig.'

'Craig and his boss.'

'It's a work thing?'

'I guess that's one way to look at it. Craig's new boss was at our house when I arrived on Friday night. I hadn't met her before and she wasn't expecting to meet me. She was wearing one of Craig's shirts and not much else. Turns out Craig is sleeping with his boss.'

'Shit.'

'It gets worse.' It was easier to talk when they were walking side by side, looking out at the ocean. Much easier than sitting opposite each other at a table. She didn't feel quite so foolish when she couldn't see his expression.

'What could be worse?'

'He's taken a new deal and he's staying in Brisbane. He's not coming to Sydney.' It was strange how easily she could talk to Ryder but had never been able to really open up with anyone else. He knew things about her that even her own siblings didn't.

'Why is that worse? You don't *want* him to move here now, do you?'

'But I'm already here. I transferred to Sydney for him. I didn't need to move.' Even though her siblings were in Sydney she hadn't really wanted to move. She hadn't wanted to leave her house.

'Being here isn't the end of the world. You have a good job and your family is here. You can stay.'

'But I had a life in Brisbane too and I gave it up for Craig. I thought I was giving it up for us, for our future together, but apparently I gave it up for nothing.'

'I understand the situation sucks and it wasn't what you expected but isn't it better to know now what sort of person he is?'

'What do you mean, "now"?'

'Before you found yourself married with a couple of kids. Being cheated on is tough but better now than after you are married. It's a lot harder to walk away then.'

'It's not that easy now.'

'Of course it is.'

'We have a house together,' she argued.

'It's just a house.'

But it was more than that to her. How did she explain that it was the thought that she might lose her house that was upsetting her more than Craig's actions? 'I can't believe that he took her home to *my* house.'

'You're more upset about *where* he cheated on you than over the fact he did cheat on you?'

Ryder's tone suggested there was something wrong with her emotionally if she was more attached to her house than to her boyfriend of almost two years. Was he right?

'He violated my privacy, my sanctuary. That's what hurts the most. I didn't want to rely on him and it turns out I shouldn't have.' By buying the house together she knew she had created a dependence on him financially but she'd thought they'd had the same end goal in sight. 'I didn't need him to love me, I just needed him to respect me.'

'Everyone needs to be loved, Poppy.'

She shook her head. 'No. Not me. I don't want to be in love. I don't want to be dependent on someone else for my emotional needs.'

She'd been right when she'd asked Lily what was wrong with them. Why they couldn't seem to have successful relationships. She blamed her parents, although she knew that was probably unfair. You needed to be brave to love because love could hurt and she suspected she wasn't brave enough.

As she tried to work out how to articulate her thoughts without making herself sound completely crazy, she felt a few spots of rain. They had turned for home but when she looked over her shoulder she could see a southerly storm front rolling in behind them.

Before she could say anything the heavens opened and within seconds they were soaked to the skin by the deluge.

Ryder grabbed her hand and even though they were already drenched, they ran for home.

Poppy changed out of her wet clothes and by the time she came back into the kitchen Ryder had stripped off his shirt and hung it over the back of a chair to dry.

Poppy swallowed, suddenly nervous and unsure where to look. She'd seen him bare-chested and semi-naked plenty of times at work over the past couple of weeks but it seemed far more intimate now in this setting. There was just two of them with nothing else to focus on. No medical emergency to draw her attention, no crowds of beachgoers.

'Would you like me to see if Lily has some of Otto's clothes in her room? You could borrow a shirt?'

'No, it's okay, my shirt won't take long to dry,' he said as he opened the fridge and pulled out a block of cheese. He looked right at home in Lily's kitchen. Anyone walking in would assume he lived there but he'd always fitted in seamlessly into their lives. Why should things be any different now?

'What are you doing?'

'I thought you'd be hungry. I'm making cheesy treats. I assume you still eat them?'

Poppy smiled. Toasted cheese sandwiches had been their go-to after school, post-surfing snack. 'They're still my favourite,' she said.

Poppy opened beers for them both, pinching them from Jet's supply, before she sat down to enjoy the view as Ryder bent over to open the oven and turn on the grill. It had always been Ryder who had made this snack for them and sitting watching him and breathing in the scent of grilled cheese transported her back through the years. To when they'd had nothing to worry about other than catching a wave or whether there was bread and cheese in the kitchen.

It was funny how she had always thought of him as Jet's friend, but revisiting the memory of those months before his family had moved away she realised now that he had spent far more time with her than he had with Jet. There had been a time when Jet had been sidelined with glandular fever and while Ryder had visited him frequently, Jet's fatigue had meant those visits had been brief and Ryder had spent more time with Poppy. Had that been a conscious action on his part? One day she might find the courage to ask him.

'Can you cook anything else or is this still your go-to?'

'Are you complaining?' He grinned at her as he slid the sandwiches out of the grill.

'Not at all. Just curious.'

'I think I'm pretty handy in the kitchen,' he said as he piled the sandwiches on a plate and took them out to the deck.

They sat in silence, eating their way through the pile of sandwiches as they watched the storm roll over the ocean.

'Feeling better?' Ryder asked when the plate was almost empty.

'A little,' she admitted.

'I know it seems bad now and you're hurting but you *will* be okay.'

'I just hate being taken for a fool.'

'Look on the bright side. I know how much you love to make plans—this is a perfect chance to make some new ones.'

Despite herself, Poppy found herself laughing.

'The future is as bright as you want to make it,' he added.

What would her future look like now?

She had assumed she and Craig would continue on as they had, happily cohabiting. But apparently there hadn't been so much of the happy. She hadn't pictured herself get-

ting married, making that sort of commitment, and Craig had never mentioned it either.
She hadn't dreamed of marriage. It wasn't as
if she'd seen many examples of happy mar-
riages. Her parents had never married and
Lily and Otto's marriage was strained, to say
the least. Even Ryder's parents were divorced.
Poppy hadn't expected or even wanted to be
married but she had expected fidelity.

She finished the last sandwich and rested
her head back on the chair.

'You look exhausted. Time for bed.'

Ryder stood and reached for her hand, pulling her to her feet. His hand was warm, his
grip gentle and comforting, and Poppy didn't
want to let go of him. Tears sprang to her
eyes as she was suddenly overwhelmed. She
wasn't sure if what she was feeling was affection for Ryder or if she was simply overcome with emotion after the events of the past
twenty-four hours but she struggled to keep
the tears from overflowing.

'Hey, it'll be okay, you'll be okay.' Ryder
wrapped her in his embrace and Poppy leaned
into him, taking solace in his strength. 'You'll
get through this.'

She stood still for a long time. She didn't
want to move, she could have stayed like that
all night, wrapped in his arms, blocking out

the world. She took a deep breath. His naked chest was warm under her cheek and she was suddenly aware of the intimacy of their posture. If she turned her face a few millimetres she would be able to press her lips against his bare skin.

'I'm here for you, okay?' he said.

Poppy looked up at him to find him watching her. She nodded and placed her hands on his chest and he relaxed his arms, allowing her freedom to move, but she wasn't intending on pushing him away and he didn't let her go.

His blue eyes were dark and intense, his expression unreadable. She stood still and silent as she watched him dip his head towards her. Suddenly his expression was completely readable, his intention clear. He moved in slow motion and she knew she could stop him at any time. But she wasn't going to do that. She didn't want to stop him.

She spread her hands apart and ran them around his back as she stepped in closer again.

'What do you need, Poppy?'

'You.' She needed him like she needed oxygen. She'd wanted him for as long as she could remember and perhaps tonight her wish would be granted.

There was no room in her head for the thoughts of the past day, there was no room for anything other than the man who stood before her, who held her as if he never wanted to let her go and looked at her as if he couldn't live without her.

'Are you sure?'

Her reply was silent. She nodded and raised herself onto her toes and pressed her mouth to his.

She heard him moan and his hands moved down below her waist. He cupped her bottom and pulled her towards him until she was pressed against his groin. She could feel his erection, strong and hard between them. He teased her lips apart with his tongue and she opened her mouth willingly, offering herself to him. All her old fantasies returned. She had dreamed of this moment many times over the years and tonight she would take the moment a step further. She wasn't going to miss her opportunity again.

CHAPTER SIX

RYDER CLOSED HIS eyes as Poppy's lips parted under his. He'd imagined having a second chance many times—was tonight it?

Her lips were soft, her mouth warm and moist. She felt good in his arms and she tasted even better.

He didn't stop to think about the wisdom of what they were doing. He didn't want to stop. Not unless she asked him to. He'd been waiting years for this moment and he'd given up thinking it would ever eventuate.

She'd had a traumatic twenty-four hours and he didn't want to take advantage of her but he did want to take her. To claim her. To have her. And if she didn't object he would have her right here, right now, on the cool tiles of the living-room floor.

He didn't want to let her go but they needed privacy as her sisters could walk in at any moment. He lifted her up and she wrapped

her legs around his waist as she clung to him.
Her arms went around his neck as he carried
her to the bedroom.

Craig was an idiot, he thought as he took
one, two, three steps across the room to reach
the bed. Did Craig have any idea what he was
throwing away?

But Ryder was grateful. Craig's actions had
given Poppy back to him and he wasn't going
to walk away again.

He stopped at the bed and Poppy slid her
legs from around his waist and stood in front
of him. He could see her pulse beating at the
base of her throat, her lips were parted, her
mouth pink and soft, her eyes gleaming.

Her fingers left his shoulders and held
the hem of her T-shirt. She tugged it over
her head, revealing creamy flesh and full,
rounded breasts.

Ryder swallowed. There was only so much
temptation he could stand. He forgot about
everything that had happened over the past
day, the past week, that past twelve years. He
only had one thought. *Get her into bed before
she comes to her senses.*

He brought his eyes back to her face. She
pinned him with her gaze but as she dropped
her T-shirt on the floor and her hands moved

lower, and he couldn't help himself. His eyes followed the path of her movements.

Her fingers undid the button on her shorts and she pushed them to the floor and stepped out of them. She stood before him wearing nothing but a bra and a pair of very skimpy briefs.

Ryder was mesmerised. His eyes travelled upwards, up the length of her bare legs, long and tanned, to her slim hips, to the tiny triangle of fabric at the junction of her thighs that was barely preserving her modesty.

He couldn't speak. A severe lack of blood to his brain had robbed him of the power of speech. But he could admire. So he did.

She was gorgeous.

His gaze travelled higher, over her flat stomach and her round belly button to her full breasts that seemed to strain against the lace of her bra.

She was perfect.

He ran his fingers up her thigh, cupping the curve of her bottom. Poppy closed her eyes and arched her hips, letting him pull her closer to him. He bent his head and kissed her. She opened her mouth, joining them together. Ryder ran his hand over her hip and up across her ribs until his fingers grazed her breast. Through the lace of her bra he felt her nipple peak under his touch. She moaned softly and reached for him but he wasn't done yet.

Her eyes were still closed as he reached behind her back. His fingers found the clasp of her bra and with a flick of his thumb he undid the fastening. Her hair tumbled over her shoulders as her breasts spilled from the lace. He pushed her hair to one side and lowered his head. He flicked his tongue over one breast, sucking it into his mouth. He heard Poppy moan as he teased her nipple with his mouth. He had one hand wrapped behind her, holding her close, and he slid his other hand down her stomach, his fingers sliding under the fabric of her briefs. His fingers slid between her thighs. She was wet and warm and felt like heaven.

'Make love to me, Ryder.'

He dropped to his knees in front of her and gently pulled her underwear down. She was shaking, unsteady on her feet. She sat on the edge of the bed as he knelt before her.

He ran one hand up the smooth skin of the inside of her thigh. Her knees were spread wide and she moaned and thrust her hips towards him as his fingers found her centre. He put his head between her thighs, replacing his fingers with his tongue. His hands went under her bottom as he lifted her to his mouth, supporting her there as his tongue darted inside her. She was slick and sweet and she moaned as he explored her inner sanctum. He enjoyed oral sex, giving and receiving, and tonight was no exception.

Poppy thrust her hips towards him again, urging him deeper. Her legs wrapped around his chest, holding him in place, not that he had plans to go anywhere. She was wet and hot, her sex swollen with desire as he tasted her and teased her, making her pant, making her beg for him.

'Ryder, please. I want you naked. I want you inside me.'

'Patience, Poppy,' he said, his voice muffled against the soft skin of her hip bone. 'Relax and enjoy, we've got all night.' He wasn't ready to stop. Not yet. He knew she was close to climaxing and he wanted to bring her to orgasm like this. He wanted to taste it, to feel it.

He ignored her request as he continued to work his magic with his tongue, licking and sucking the swollen bud of her desire. He continued until Poppy had forgotten her request, until she had forgotten everything except her own satisfaction.

'Yes, yes… Oh, Ryder, don't stop.'

He had no intention of stopping. He heard her sharp little intake of breath and then she began to shudder.

'Yes. Oh, Ryder.'

She buried her fingers in his hair and clamped her thighs around his shoulders as she came. Shuddering and gasping before she collapsed, relaxed and spent.

'God, you're good at that,' she said, and he could hear the smile and contentment in her voice.

'Thank you.' He stood up from his knees and lay alongside her on the bed, his hand resting on her stomach as she cuddled into him.

'Now will you get naked?' she asked. He turned his head to look at her. 'It's your turn,' she said. 'I want to feel you inside me.'

Poppy watched as Ryder's blue eyes darkened. They were a dark navy now, the brightness overcome with lust and desire. She felt a surge of power, knowing that he wanted her as much as she wanted him. She slipped her fingers under the waistband of his jeans. She could see he wanted to give in.

'Please?' she begged.

'Seeing as you asked so nicely,' he replied with a grin as he flicked open the button of his jeans.

Poppy took charge. She sat up and pushed him onto his back, tugging his jeans over his hips as she undressed him. His boxer shorts came off with his jeans and as his erection sprang free Poppy's groin flooded with heat. She straddled him, trapping him between her thighs. She cupped his testes and then encircled his shaft with her hand. It was thick and hard and warm and pulsed with a life of its own as she ran her hand up its length. She rolled her fingers over the end and coaxed the moisture from his body. Ryder gasped and his body shook with lust.

'In my wallet,' he panted. 'I have protection.'

Ryder's jeans were lying on the floor. Poppy stretched to her right and lifted them to the bed. She found his wallet in the front pocket. She flicked it open and pulled out a condom. She tore open the packet and rolled the sheath down over him.

She was still sitting across his thighs and Ryder's eyes darkened further as she brought herself forward and raised herself up onto her knees. She put her hands either side of his head and kept her eyes on his face as she lifted herself up and took his length inside her. He closed his eyes and she watched him breathe in deeply as her flesh encased him, joining them together.

She filled herself with his length before lifting her weight from him. She lifted herself up again, and down, as Ryder held onto her hips and started to time her thrusts, matching their rhythms together. Slow at first and then gradually faster. And faster. Poppy tried to stay in charge but she found it impossible to control her body. All she could think of was how good this felt and that she wanted more. And more.

She let him take control. His thumbs were on the front of her hips, his fingers behind her pelvis as he guided her up and down, matching her rhythm to his thrusts, each movement bringing her closer to climax.

She liked this position. She liked being able to watch him, she liked being able to see him getting closer and closer to release. His lips were parted, his breathing was rapid and shallow, his thrusts getting faster. She spread her knees, letting him deeper inside her until she had taken all of him. Her body was flooded with heat. Every nerve ending was crying out for his touch. 'Now, Ryder. Now.'

He opened his eyes and his gaze locked with hers as he took her to the top of the peak. Her body started to quiver and just when she didn't think she could stand it any longer she felt Ryder shudder. She held her breath as he thrust into her and she could feel his release as he came inside her, claiming her as they climaxed together.

Completely spent and satisfied, she collapsed onto him, covering his body with hers. Their skin felt warm and flushed from their efforts and they were both panting as he wrapped his arms around her back, holding her to him. She could feel his heart beating under her chest. She could feel it as its rhythm slowed, gradually returning to normal.

She closed her eyes and lay quietly, listening to the sound of Ryder's breathing.

For once in her life she had completely let herself lose control and it felt good.

She had never given herself over so totally to someone else or to her desires. Tonight had been a long time coming and she didn't regret a second of it.

Maybe Craig had done her a favour. Ryder certainly had.

She smiled.

'What's that smile for?' Ryder asked.

She opened her eyes and found him watching her. 'I didn't know sex could be like that.'

When she'd been in relationships, more often than not she'd had sex because she'd known it was expected of her but she'd never felt a desperate burning desire for it. Unless, it seemed, Ryder was around.

'It was pretty amazing,' he agreed.

'It was incredible.' She'd had good sex but she'd never experienced mind-blowing sex. Until now.

'There's more where that came from,' he said as he pressed his lips against the soft skin at the base of her throat.

Poppy's smile widened as his fingers trailed over her hip bone and slid between her thighs and she forgot all about feeling obliged to have sex and focussed instead on the bliss of making love.

Poppy woke to the sound of a text message.

She opened her eyes, expecting to see Ryder in the bed next to her before remembering that he'd left in the early hours of the morning. She bit back her disappointment. She'd wanted him to stay but he hadn't wanted to run into her sisters.

She hoped that had been his only reason for leaving. She hoped he didn't think they'd made a mistake. Hoped he wasn't regretting what they'd done.

She scolded herself as she reached over to pick up her phone. As usual she was over-thinking things and assuming the worst. Her mood lifted when she saw his message on the screen.

Are you awake?

She was smiling as she dialled his number. 'Good morning,' she said when he answered. 'I'm awake now. Where are you?'

'I'm out the front. Grab your board and your wetsuit. We're going surfing.'

Poppy's heart skipped a beat. He obviously wasn't having second thoughts.

She quickly pulled on her swimsuit, brushed her teeth and grabbed her gear. She closed the front door quietly. Ryder was waiting on the kerb. He greeted her with a kiss and took her surfboard, sliding it into the back of his car next to his.

'How did you sleep?' he asked her as he drove her down to Bronte Beach.

'Like a baby.' She'd expected to have a restless night, she'd expected that her mind would be spinning as she processed what had happened with Craig, but Ryder had managed to distract her completely in the most delightful of ways.

'No regrets?'

She smiled. 'None. Why?'

'I was worried you might be feeling like we rushed things a bit.'

'No.' She shook her head as she wondered if she should tell him that she'd been waiting twelve years for last night to happen. That could hardly be called rushing things. 'You?'

'Maybe.'

'Oh.' She didn't like the sound of that.

'Don't get me wrong, I enjoyed every minute of it but you have to admit we didn't really think things through. I didn't give you a chance to process what had happened with Craig. You haven't had a chance to decide if you want to work things out.'

'Trust me, I don't.' Her relationship with Craig was well and truly over. She couldn't forgive infidelity and after last night there was no way she was ever going to settle for average sex again.

It was a glorious morning. The beach was bathed in pink light and the ocean was warm. She didn't want to think about Craig. She knew they would have things to sort out but that could wait. She blocked all thoughts of Craig from her mind. 'Is that all that was bothering you?' she asked, as they paddled out past the break.

'No.'

What more could there be? she thought nervously. 'Oh? What else is there?'

'I need to know if last night was just a one-off.'

Poppy's heart plummeted in her chest. Was that what he wanted? She was almost afraid to ask but she had to know. She swallowed the lump in her throat and said, 'Is that what you thought? Is that all you wanted?'

'What! No, not at all. I just needed to know if last night was just a reaction to Craig's behaviour or if it was more serious. I don't want to get caught in the middle and I don't want to be your rebound guy.'

Poppy could breathe again. 'You're not.'

Ryder sat up on his board and the morning sun caught his hair, turning the tips golden. His skin was bronzed and the water droplets on his shoulders glistened in the morning light. He looked like a Greek god and Poppy's breath caught in her throat and her insides wobbled. He was divine, inside and out, and she couldn't believe she'd finally managed to fulfil her teenage fantasy. She had enjoyed every minute of it and fully intended to do it again.

'I have been waiting for last night for twelve years,' she told him as she pushed herself into a sitting position and let her legs dangle in the water. 'It definitely wasn't a re-bound thing.'

'Good,' he said as he reached for her board. He pulled her closer until their knees were touching and leaned towards her. He lifted his hand and slid his fingers under her hair, cupping the back of her head. She lifted her chin and his lips brushed her mouth.

She closed her eyes and parted her lips as he kissed her. He tasted salty and warm. She kissed him back, savouring the feel of his hands on her skin, his mouth on hers.

A small wave rocked her board. She opened her eyes and grabbed his forearms for support as she regained her balance.

Ryder ran his thumb along her jaw to the edge of her mouth and Poppy would have sworn she could feel the zing of awareness spread right through her from her lips to her toes. She sighed and sucked his thumb into her mouth.

'Where do we go from here?' he asked.

She took his hand, holding it in both of hers. 'I'm not sure.' She hadn't thought about what would happen next. She'd only got as far as last night.

'You don't have a plan?' He was smiling. Teasing her.

She shook her head. 'I just want to enjoy this.' Whatever *this* was.

He was watching her closely and she wondered if he knew what she was thinking. He usually did, but she couldn't help her fears. It was too soon to tell him how she felt. She couldn't do it.

She was scared of verbalising her feelings but she knew she needed to try to explain her thoughts to him. 'Whenever I make relationship plans, things go awry. Can we just spend some time together and see what happens?'

He nodded. 'Sure. If that's what you want.'

She appreciated that he didn't push her for more. She didn't want to make promises neither of them might be able to keep. It was better not to expect too much. She didn't want to be disappointed.

He knew the conversation was done for now and she watched him as he caught a wave. He carved up the ocean, his powerful legs working the board. She almost blushed when she thought that just last night she'd been tangled up in his legs. Just last night those powerful thighs had been between hers, taking her to places she'd only ever dreamed of.

She would enjoy this, enjoy him, she decided, for as long as it lasted.

* * *

Ryder dropped Poppy home after a post-surfing breakfast before he headed to work. Lily was lying on the couch and she closed her laptop and sat up when Poppy came into the lounge.

'You're looking better than I expected given the nasty surprise you copped,' she said. 'How are you feeling?'

'Great.'

'Really?'

'Yep.' Poppy could feel the enormous grin she had plastered on her face but she couldn't help it.

'And would your good mood have anything to do with Ryder?'

'What makes you say that?'

'I thought I saw him leaving here in the early hours of the morning.'

'You saw him? He didn't say anything.'

'He looked like he had his mind on other things. Are you going to tell me what's going on?'

'You asked him to pick me up from the airport.' Poppy sat on the couch next to her sister.

'This was hours later.'

'We went for a walk, he made me dinner...'

'And then?'

'I slept with him.'

'Oh, my God! Poppy! You don't think it's a bit soon to be jumping into bed with someone else? You've only just broken up with Craig.'

Poppy hadn't meant to say anything, not just yet, but her excited mood made her accidentally verbose. 'I didn't realise there was a rule.'

'There's not a rule exactly but most people I know wait a few days, not hours.'

Again, she felt like she'd been waiting twelve years for last night. In her opinion she'd done her time and she hadn't been willing to wait one more minute for what had turned out to be the most amazing experience of her life. But she wasn't about to tell Lily all of that. It was a little too revealing. 'It was just a bit of fun,' she said instead.

Lily raised one eyebrow. 'A bit of fun is revenge sex with a hot stranger. Sex that makes you think you're still desirable after your boyfriend cheats on you. It is *not* having sex with a guy you've known for years. A guy who you had a teenage crush on but who is first and foremost a friend. Someone you'll still have to see if things go pear-shaped!'

'I can handle it.'

'Are you sure? What's your plan?'

'My plan? I don't have one.'

Lily looked at her like she didn't recognise her and Poppy could understand that. She always had a plan but she'd got carried away last night. She'd let her hormones get the better of her and she'd slept with Ryder because she'd wanted to and before she could think about what came next. Now she just wanted to enjoy herself. She didn't want to make plans.

She'd never experienced anything like last night and she couldn't have planned it better if she'd tried, so that was her lesson. No plans.

'You've had a crush on Ryder for years,' Lily said. 'Can you handle a casual fling? I don't want you to get your heart broken.'

Poppy hadn't said anything about a casual fling. That wasn't where her mind was at but she was keeping that to herself. 'I know you like to protect us all but you don't need to worry. I'll be fine.'

Her boyfriend of two years had just cheated on her and she felt fine. Better than fine. She felt great. Craig's infidelity hadn't broken her heart and she didn't think Ryder would either. She could handle this.

For the next week Poppy thought she was handling things perfectly. She was taking things one day at a time, no plans, no expectations. It was very unlike her, this casual approach, but she was happy just spending time with Ryder. She'd wanted this chance for as long as she could remember and she was determined to enjoy it.

Work and Ryder were keeping her busy, which was good. It meant there was no time to spend thinking about Craig and the things they had to sort out. Poppy wanted to ignore that for as long as possible. She wanted to think only happy thoughts. She wanted to think about Ryder.

They spent almost every minute together when they weren't working—surfing, sharing meals and making love. Poppy was still blown away by how amazing the sex was. How had she never known it could be like that?

Maybe letting go was the secret.

Maybe Ryder was the secret.

Her muscles were still aching from the last session just half an hour ago and she was smiling as Ryder found them an empty table at Lao Lao's Kitchen. Poppy had wanted to stay in bed and order takeaway, but Ryder had insisted they go out and this restaurant was quickly becoming their favourite.

'Thank you, An Na,' Poppy said as the young girl brought their final dish. She cleared their empty plates as Ryder waved at someone across the restaurant.

Poppy turned back towards the door and saw a fit, athletic-looking brunette walking towards them.

'Hi, Steph, what are you doing here?' Ryder greeted her.

'Picking up a takeaway.'

'Steph, this is Poppy Carlson, Jet's sister. Poppy, this is Steph, one of the injured lifeguards.'

Ryder's introduction left Poppy a little disheartened. Was that all she was to him still? Jet's sister? She realised she wanted him to see her as someone more, someone important. A girlfriend. A partner. But was that fair? She was the one who hadn't wanted to make plans, hadn't wanted commitment. She couldn't expect one thing from him if she wasn't prepared to give him the same. She was scared to commit to a relationship officially. Relationships never worked out for her. If she wasn't committing in public she could pretend she wasn't committing in private.

But she knew that was a lie.

Despite what she'd told Lily, she was scared Ryder would leave her and break her heart in the process. She was scared he wouldn't love her.

Realising her musings were making her appear rude, she dragged her focus back to the conversation. 'How's your recovery going?' she asked, just as Steph's name was called.

'Slowly,' Steph replied as she glanced back over her shoulder. 'That's my order,' she said. 'Ryder can fill you in. Enjoy your dinner.'

'Which one was she?' Poppy asked as Steph returned to the counter. 'The fractured scapula?' she guessed. The other lifeguard had undergone a knee reconstruction and given the time frame Poppy thought Steph was far too mobile to be the post-op knee patient.

Ryder nodded.

'How long has she been off for?'

'I'm not a hundred per cent sure but I know she's keen to come back. She had a fitness test today.'

'How did she go?'

'I gather she struggled with some of the strength components. She couldn't pull the dummy out of the water.'

Poppy knew one of the tests was retrieving a forty-kilogram dummy and wrangling it onto a rescue board. Managing the dead weight was difficult at the best of times, let alone after a fractured shoulder blade.

'There was a bit of discussion about finding her some suitable light duties but until she can handle all the physical components of the job she's not going to be fully cleared. It'll be another few weeks at least.'

'So you'll be around for a bit longer?'

'You're not keen to get rid of me, are you?'

'Not yet. But when Steph is cleared? What will that mean for you? Will you continue on your gap year?'

She knew Ryder's contract was only temporary. He was covering sick leave and once those lifeguards returned to duty his contract would be over. She had no idea what his plans were after that. And suddenly her idea of going with the flow, of not planning for the future, seemed less solid. Ryder might be gone before she knew it. And what would she do then?

He was shaking his head. 'I've just about run out of time. I'll be heading home at the end of summer.'

'Back to Perth?' Poppy didn't want to think of him leaving her again, moving back across the country just like he had twelve years before.

He nodded.

'To do what? Work as a lifeguard?'

'Is there something wrong with that?'

Poppy could hear she'd offended him but

surely that wasn't his career plan? 'You don't think you'll get bored?'

'Have you had the same conversation with Jet? Does he seem bored to you?'

'He's still competing in the Ironman series,' she countered. 'I don't think he's planning on being a lifeguard for ever.'

'You don't think. But it is possible. Several of the guys have been full-time lifeguards for years. There's good job satisfaction.'

'But not great pay.'

'It's not all about the money for me, Poppy. Some things are more important.'

Poppy would disagree but she thought it was wiser to stay silent.

'Don't stress,' he said. 'I have a plan. Are you working tomorrow?'

'No.' It had become her habit to volunteer for any available overtime shifts as she'd been eager for the extra income to put towards her house in Brisbane, but for the past week she hadn't put her hand up for additional hours but had chosen to spend the time with Ryder instead.

'Meet me at the North Bondi lifeguard tower at four and I'll show you my plan,' he said.

Poppy could see Ryder sitting in the sand at the base of the tower at the northern end of the beach. He was surrounded by half a dozen teenagers and as many surfboards. He was dressed in a pair of boardshorts and a T-shirt. His knees were bent and he rested his elbow on his knees, the T-shirt pulled tight across his back and sculpted to his arms, showcasing his muscles. He looked good, almost as good with a shirt on as without, she decided, and the thought made her smile.

She wondered what he was doing here. He was dressed in casual clothes, not his lifeguard uniform, and he was obviously not on duty. Giving surfing lessons perhaps? Was that his plan—to become a surf instructor? In her opinion that showed even less ambition than being a professional lifeguard *and* had less job security. Having grown up with a father who was a surf instructor, she knew that from personal experience.

Ryder had so much to offer the world and she knew she'd be disappointed if she found out that he wasn't going to challenge himself. The teenage Ryder had never backed away from a challenge. He'd been determined, bold and confident. She hoped that was still the case but this time she wouldn't leap to conclusions. He had promised to tell her his plan and she would listen first. This time she wouldn't make assumptions and she wouldn't judge.

Ryder and the kids were sitting in a semi-circle around a pile of hot chips, which were spread out on a square of white butcher's paper. They were eating and chatting but Ryder stood up as she reached them. 'Hey.'

She thought he was going to greet her with a kiss but he simply gestured to the kids. 'Guys, this is Poppy. I thought she could join us for a surf today.'

They sat in the sand and he went around the group and introduced the kids to her. There was a mixture of girls and boys and Poppy guessed them to be aged between fifteen and eighteen. They were a disparate group and she couldn't quite work out what they were doing with Ryder.

'Are you hungry?' he asked. 'Help yourself.'

Poppy reached for a chip as the conversation continued around her. She enjoyed watching him interact with the kids. There was nothing stilted or forced about his demeanour, he was completely relaxed and the kids were obviously just as comfortable with him.

'How do you know Easy?' one of the boys asked as Poppy munched on a chip.

Poppy wasn't sure how to answer. Did she say they were old friends? Worked together?

Were sleeping together? That last description, while true, probably wasn't an appropriate response.

'Poppy is a paramedic,' Ryder replied before she could decide what to say. 'She works here at Bondi.'

'Cool.'

She wondered why Ryder hadn't said they were dating. Had it just been a bit of casual fun in his mind? Something to pass the time until he went back to Perth? She wished she could tell what he was thinking as easily as he seemed to be able to read her mind.

She knew she was being contradictory. She was the one who had insisted on keeping things casual. On not making plans. She knew it wasn't fair of her to want Ryder to be more invested in things than she was. It wasn't fair to expect him to risk his heart but when was life ever fair? She didn't want him to be able to walk away from her easily. She didn't want to be rejected by him.

'I couldn't handle all that blood.' The kids all chimed in, commenting on her choice of career and bringing her mind back to the present.

'What's the grossest thing you've seen?' one asked.

'You, Jase!' one of the boys teased.

'Tyler!' Ryder's voice was quiet but firm and Poppy could tell he was not pleased.

Tyler could obviously tell too. 'I was just kidding,' he said with a sheepish expression.

'Kidding around is fine but it's not okay to make jokes at the expense of others. You know our rules, Tyler.'

'Sorry, Easy. Sorry, Jase,' he apologised.

Jase and Ryder both nodded in acknowledgement before Jase asked again. 'Will you tell us?'

'You know the thing that grosses me out the most?' Poppy said. The boys all leaned in to hear her answer while most of the girls looked a little more hesitant. 'I can handle the broken bones and the blood but the worst is when people vomit. Especially if they vomit on me.'

'Yuck.'

'That is *so* gross.'

'Told you.' She smiled. 'And that happens a lot. Most of what I do isn't gross. There are some car accidents but there are more heart attacks and getting pregnant women in labour to hospital. Around here there are skateboarding injuries, surfing injuries and near-drownings.'

'It's kinda cool you get to save lives.'

'Yeah, it's pretty cool,' Poppy admitted.

She loved her job. It was everything she'd
hoped for and one of her favourite things was
how confident she felt in herself when she
was in uniform. She felt strong and capable
but it seemed like the kids had heard enough
from her. They had devoured the food and
were now getting to their feet, ready to hit
the water.

'Are you coming for a surf, Easy?' Jase
asked.

'In a bit.'

'You don't want to surf?' she asked as the
kids grabbed their boards and ran down to
the water.

'I'd rather sit here and talk to you,' he replied as he reached for her hand. 'I can't do
that out there.'

She looked down at their hands, at their
intertwined fingers. Her body sprang to life
at the slightest touch from Ryder and her reaction scared her. Being with him felt right,
it felt perfectly natural, and she knew she'd
been waiting for him all her life, but she was
finding herself constantly on edge too, waiting for him to walk away. Waiting for him to
leave. She hated that feeling but she couldn't
divest herself of it. She was trying her best
to ignore it but it wasn't easy.

'Who are those kids?' she asked, trying to

keep her mind occupied. She had a fair idea but what she didn't know was how and why Ryder was involved.

'They're a group of at-risk teenagers I've been volunteering with through the local council. I offered to teach them to surf.'

'Why?'

'They've all had, or are having, tough times. They've experienced bullying or abuse or have been diagnosed with depression or anxiety. Exercise benefits their mental health and builds confidence. Teaching them to surf was something I could do and it gives them an escape as well as a network, a social support group if you like, along with some fresh air and exercise. It's a win-win for everyone mostly. I reckon I get as much out of it as they do.'

'I didn't know that was something you were interested in.' He was a natural with the kids. He'd always been a good listener; she'd never found him to be judgemental and it seemed the kids recognised that too. 'Why did you get involved?'

'When I came to Bondi one of the first jobs I did as a lifeguard was dealing with the aftermath of a suicide. Back in Perth I had some experience with people who were battling anxiety and depression and I decided I wanted to make a difference. This was one way of doing that.'

'What happened in Perth?'

'Mum and Lucy both battled depression but they dealt with it in different ways. Lucy developed an eating disorder and Mum was too busy numbing her loss with alcohol to notice.'

'And now? How are they doing now?'

'Much better. It's taken a while, though, and it was hard initially, there was a lot of baggage to sort through. To be honest, I think Lucy's problems started before we'd even left Byron. It was a cry for attention but no one noticed. Mum and Dad were too busy fighting and I was too busy trying to stay out of the way. It was only later that I felt there was more I could have done to help Lucy. More I *should* have done. At the time I was too focussed on myself. I was seventeen, I just wanted to get out of the house and spend time with you.'

'With me?'

'I was happy at your house. There was no fighting, no arguing.'

Poppy agreed there had been few arguments but in her opinion it had been because no one had taken responsibility for anything in the commune, including responsibility for the children. Life had just drifted along and the kids had learned to organise themselves. The kids had been left to their own devices, no curfews, no supervision, no boundaries and very few disagreements. Any arguments had to be sorted out amongst themselves. They might not have been showered with love and affection but they learned resilience.

But Poppy felt dreadful. She'd had no idea what he'd been going through. She'd never thought about what it must have been like at home for him. 'Ryder, I had no idea. I'm so sorry. I should have listened.'

'I didn't want to talk about it. I just wanted to get away, to pretend it wasn't happening, and being at your place gave me the chance to do that. Until the day that my mother announced we were leaving. Then there was no escaping reality and it hit us with a vengeance once we got to Perth. It was only then, when I spent more time at home, that I saw what was going on with Lucy. Her anxiety escalated as Mum's depression worsened. It was a cry for attention from Lucy but Mum didn't notice. She was dealing with her own pain. It was up to me to figure out how to get them through that.'

'But who looked after you? You were only a teenager yourself.'

He shrugged, dismissing her concerns. 'I

was okay. But that's why I know what these kids are dealing with. I figure I can make a difference. This is what I want to do. Work with disadvantaged or troubled kids. I told you I had a plan—this is it.'

'So what exactly are you going to do?'

'I've already done it. You're looking at a newly qualified psychologist.'

'What? Why didn't you tell me?'

'When you were telling me off for having no aspirations, you mean?'

He was smiling at her but Poppy was embarrassed. She felt remorseful but somewhat vindicated. 'Well, I was right, wasn't I? You *do* want more. But if you have a psychology degree...' She trailed off, not wanting to say the wrong thing again.

'Why am I goofing around in Bondi?' Ryder finished. He'd always known what she was thinking. 'I only finished my degree in the middle of the year. I had to work while I was studying so I could only study part time, but Mum and Lucy are both doing okay now. That's why I could take off. This was my time.'

'So what comes next?'

'I've got a job offer in Perth, a graduate psychologist position, working with kids. I start in February.'

'So you're definitely leaving.'

He nodded and Poppy realised her fears were real. He had plans that didn't include her. He would leave her and she'd be alone again.

She had assumed this thing between them wouldn't, couldn't, last. She'd known it was only a matter of time before things went wrong, before Ryder would realise there was something wrong with her, that she wasn't worthy of love, but it looked like he might be gone sooner than she'd expected, and despite what she'd told Lily she knew her heart would crumble when he left.

CHAPTER SEVEN

RYDER CHECKED THE TIME. Four hours left of his shift. Four hours until he would be on his way to collect Poppy. He used to look forward to the end of his shift so that he could go for a surf. Now he looked forward to seeing Poppy.

They had spent years apart but he'd never forgotten her, and while she was still the girl of his teenage fantasies, time had marked her. She was still gorgeous, she still set his pulse racing, still made him lose his mind, but part of the girl he remembered had got lost in an adult world. He supposed the same could be said of all of them.

Was it unfair to compare teenage Poppy with adult Poppy? Probably. Life changed people. But Poppy had changed more than he would have expected.

She'd always had plans but her plans seemed a little one-dimensional to him. He knew she would argue that she was focussed but he would debate that she was ignoring her emotional needs in deference to her financial ones. While he understood her need for stability and security, he didn't think that fulfilment lay in material possessions.

In his opinion fulfilment came from personal connections, from having your emotional and physical needs met. And at the heart of all that was love. Not money. He was determined to convince her that financial security was not the be all and end all. Emotional security, happiness, trust and love were all far more important.

He knew Poppy's parents, and particularly her mother, hadn't been overly affectionate and that, as a consequence, she guarded her heart. He knew she loved her siblings, but could she love him?

Poppy never talked about her feelings. None of the Carlson siblings had ever spent much time talking about their feelings— their opinions, sure, but not their emotions. As a teenage boy he hadn't wanted to talk about feelings either, he'd been content just to have Poppy's company. Now he wanted her to open up to him. He knew she found it hard. He knew she was scared and vulnerable and Craig's infidelity hadn't helped. It had felt like a betrayal of the worst kind. Craig had rejected her. He hadn't loved her.

Poppy had told him she hadn't loved Craig either but that didn't take away her greatest fear. Her fear of not being loved. She'd never admitted that to him but he knew that was it. After all these years he still felt like he sometimes knew her better than she knew herself.

And he knew he had to convince her that there was more to life than a house and a healthy bank balance. He had to convince her that she needed more. Deserved more.

She needed love.

She deserved love.

His ego told him that he was the one who could give her that. He was the one who could make her happy. But was he kidding himself? Could she love him?

Ryder was starting to feel a sense of urgency. Poppy was refusing to discuss the future with him and that worried him. She always had a plan. Was she refusing to discuss her plans because they didn't include him?

Did she want to be with him or was she deliberately putting up barriers? What if, after all these years, he was just her rebound guy?

It was a possibility. She'd said she'd imagined being with him since she was sixteen but what if, after all those years, it was simply a case of him being in the right place at the right time as her relationship with Craig had imploded. Was that all this was? A matter of convenience?

Did it matter if he was the rebound guy?

He knew it did. At least to him.

He wanted a lifetime. He wanted the dream.

But was it just that? A dream. Not a reality. Not *their* reality?

He had to convince her they were meant to be together. They'd lost twelve years. He couldn't let her go now.

His time in Bondi was drawing closer to an end but as his departure date loomed he realised he didn't want to leave. Not without Poppy.

He was hoping to convince her that she could come with him. That she could make a home with him.

He still loved her, had never *stopped* loving her. Could she love him?

He hated this feeling of insecurity, hated this feeling of the unknown. He had to get her to talk to him. He had to know what she was thinking. What she was feeling. Had to know if he could be the one for her.

He knew she needed stability and security. She wanted a house, a home, and he wanted to give her that. He doubted he'd be able to convince her to move away from her siblings, but he didn't have to go back to Western Australia. He could stay here, he would stay here, he'd do it for her. He would prove to her that she was worthy of being loved, of being adored. He wouldn't let her down.

She needed him to be mature. Dependable. Reliable. Stable. She needed him to be all those things. He knew it, even if she didn't.

He would show her he could be all those things. That he could be everything she needed. And if she wasn't going to make plans, he would. He'd give it everything he had.

Ryder took a deep breath as he parked outside Poppy's house after his shift. This was it. The moment of truth.

He had booked a weekend away for the two of them, and they were headed to a bed and breakfast at a Hunter Valley winery. They would go wine tasting and walking. They'd make love, sleep late and have breakfast in bed. They could spend time together, make new memories and see what their future held.

He was smiling as he knocked on the door but his smile didn't last long.

She answered the door dressed in her paramedic's uniform.

'Did you have a shift today?' he asked. He hadn't realised she'd been rostered on.

'No.'

She looked worried, distracted. He could always tell when she had something on her mind and knew he would probably need to prise it out of her. She never willingly disclosed her feelings.

'What's happened?'

'I just got off the phone from Craig,' she said as she headed for the kitchen.

Ryder's heart raced in his chest as he followed her through to the deck. He knew it was over between Poppy and Craig but he couldn't help the feeling of jealousy that flared up against his will whenever he thought of Poppy with Craig. The mention of his name reminded Ryder of all the time Poppy had wasted on someone who didn't appreciate her.

'He wants to put the house on the market,' Poppy continued.

'That's good.' Relief washed over him. Selling the house would sever their last connection. Poppy could be done with Craig and move on. It was a good thing in his opinion but Poppy's face suggested she didn't agree. 'Isn't it?'

She was shaking her head. 'No. I don't want to sell it.'

Ryder frowned. If she didn't want to sell it could only mean one thing. 'You want to keep it?'

She nodded.

That made no sense to him. Why would she want to keep a house she'd bought with Craig? There could only be one reason. 'Are you going back to Brisbane?'

'No. I'm not planning on going back but I worked hard for that house.'

'I understand that. But it's just a house.'

'It's more than that,' she said. 'It's the first house I ever owned. It's my home. I've never felt like I've had a home before.'

'What about where you grew up?'

'The commune!? You remember what that was like? People drifted in and out of the houses as they pleased. It never felt like our house belonged to us and I want a place that I *know* is mine. My parents never owned that house, they didn't even own the land it was on, and we could have been kicked off at any time and left with nothing. I need to know I have a roof over my head and I've worked hard to get that and I'm not going to give it up.'

'What are you saying?'

'I don't want to sell. I want to buy Craig out. Which means I need all the money I can get.'

Ryder finally caught up. 'You're taking an extra shift? Tonight?'

She nodded. 'Yes.'

'What about our weekend away?'

'I'm sorry, Ryder, I need the money. I want to keep my house.'

Ryder could see his plans evaporating before him bur perhaps he could salvage something, he thought as he quickly ran through his options.

They could leave later. It would mean they lost a day but that was better than nothing. He was prepared to compromise. That was what love was all about, wasn't it? And he loved her. He suspected he'd never stopped loving her.

'Do you want to leave tomorrow instead?' he asked.

She shook her head. 'I've taken a shift tomorrow, too.'

'You're going to work all weekend?' She wouldn't look at him and he knew the answer. 'So we're not going away.'

'Can I take a rain check?'

He was beginning to suspect that life with Poppy might be an endless series of rain checks. Love was about compromise, respect, trust and honesty but Ryder didn't want to always be the only one making sacrifices, he didn't want to be the one always waiting. 'What's more important?' he asked. 'Being happy or working yourself to the bone?'

'I've put hours and hours of my time into that house, not to mention blood, sweat and tears and thousands of dollars. I'm not giving it up.'

He knew Poppy needed security and stability but he'd hoped their relationship might have been a higher priority than a house, but he'd obviously been kidding himself. 'There's more to life than a big bank balance and a fancy house, Poppy.'

If she didn't realise that then he had nothing to offer her.

His heart was heavy in his chest, his hopes and dreams dashed. Had he made a mistake? Had he let his memories could his judgement? Had the girl he remembered changed that much?

No, the Poppy he remembered was still there. Still making plans. The only problem was her current plan was to save her house at the expense of everything else.

He had plans too but it seemed that while

he was considering a future with her, she was on a different path. Did he even matter?

Ryder was nursing a mild hangover courtesy of Jet, but he knew his lack of focus was related more to Poppy than to the beers he'd had last night.

After Poppy had cancelled their plans he'd gone directly to Jet and put his hand up for any extra shifts that were available. Jet had known about his plans for the weekend but he hadn't questioned him. He'd taken one look at him and said he'd see what he could do and he'd managed to find additional shifts. Ryder appreciated the opportunity to stay busy but even though it was a glorious November day not even the brilliant sunshine could lift his mood.

Poppy had called him twice last night but he'd let the calls go through to his message service. He didn't know if he wanted to hear what she had to say. He didn't trust himself not to lose his temper. He had always prided himself on being impartial, on being able to listen to other's points of view without judgement, but Poppy was testing his patience.

He wanted to be there for her but he also wanted her to give him the same consideration. He wanted to be important to her.

He didn't want to be a stopgap, something or someone to be discarded the moment another priority came along. He wanted to be her priority.

Was he being unfair?

He didn't think so. Their relationship was fledgling but that didn't mean it wasn't important. It didn't mean he wasn't important.

If it had been any other weekend he would probably have been more understanding but this weekend was supposed to have been special and it hurt to think that Poppy could so easily give it up. Give him up.

She'd told him that she'd thought about being with him for twelve years. Now that she'd ticked that box, was she moving on? Was he nothing but a curiosity? A teenage fantasy that hadn't lived up to her expectations?

He'd been watching the water at the south end of the beach as his mind turned over. In front of him was a group of teenage boys, tackling each other and doing somersaults over the waves. He could remember doing the same thing in his youth but now, with the wisdom of experience, seeing these antics worried him. What if one of them mistimed his landing? Misjudged the depth of the water? Landed on their head? He thought of all the things that could go wrong but knew they wouldn't listen to his warnings. Knew they would consider him to be worrying over nothing.

He redirected his gaze, looking towards Backpackers' Rip, looking for anything out of the ordinary. The late afternoon swell was picking up, the breeze was coming in. He could see a lone swimmer getting close to the rip. A man with dark hair. He disappeared briefly behind a wave and Ryder waited for his head to bob up again. He didn't look like a confident swimmer and he made a note to keep an eye on him.

'Would you mind if we took a photo with you?'

Ryder's attention was drawn away from the ocean by two tourists, two pretty girls in bikinis, who brandished a cellphone. The lifeguards were constantly being asked to pose for photographs. Ryder didn't usually mind, it was a pleasant part of the job—unless the tourists got a little too familiar, which happened on occasion. This time, though, it was a couple of quick selfies and he was happy to oblige.

The girls checked the photos and, as they requested 'just one more', Ryder thought he saw a hand raised in the ocean.

He checked for the lone swimmer.

He couldn't see him.

The afternoon sun was behind him, bright on the water, and he wasn't one hundred per cent certain of what he'd seen. Maybe the swimmer had got out of the water. Maybe he hadn't seen a hand. It could have been a trick of the light. The sea was getting rough and the swell and the sunlight made it difficult to get a clear visual. But he needed to check.

He excused himself from the tourists and grabbed the binoculars and the radio. He'd call it into the Tower. Jet had a better vantage point from up there, he'd be able to see over the waves.

'Central, this is Ryder.'

'Go ahead, Easy.'

'I'm down at Backpackers'. I've had my eye on a lone swimmer, just north of the rip, behind the first breakers. I've lost sight of him behind the waves. Can you see if you can spot him? Male, dark hair.'

Ryder waited several seconds, knowing that Jet would be taking his time, scanning the waves, giving himself time to see if the swimmer was moving or giving him time to surface if he'd gone under. Looking for anything untoward. Ryder kept his eyes on the water too but came up with nothing.

'Nothing,' came Jet's reply. 'I can't see anyone on their own or anyone who looks like they're in trouble.'

Despite Jet confirming that he hadn't seen anything either, Ryder still felt uneasy. He knew it was possible that the man had returned to shore or was swimming with friends but he had the distinct impression that the man wasn't a strong swimmer and his sudden disappearance had him worried.

'I reckon I'll go out for a look,' he told Jet. 'Just to be on the safe side.'

'Copy that,' came the reply.

He lifted the rescue board from the rack on the side of the buggy and jogged into the water. He threw the board in front of him and leapt on, paddling out, up and over the swell. He didn't see anyone who looked in need of help on his way out and when he got to the spot where he'd last seen the man there was nothing but empty water. He sat astride the board and scanned the sea again. Nothing.

He paddled a little further out to check with the surfers. He knew they often came to the aid of struggling swimmers, and even though he couldn't see anyone who looked like they were being a Good Samaritan, they might be able to shed some light on the man's where-

abouts. But none of them had noticed anything untoward either.

He figured the swimmer must have left the
water while he'd been busy with the tourists. Maybe he'd imagined the hand in the
air. Maybe he hadn't seen anything at all, he
thought as he returned to the beach.

He spent the next hour patrolling the beach,
pulling people out of the water, reuniting kids
with their distracted parents, and he'd almost
forgotten about the lone swimmer when a
young woman approached the buggy where
he and Bluey were standing.

Ryder initially thought she was also after
a photo but then he saw she wasn't smiling
or holding a cellphone. She looked worried.

'Please, can you help me?' She spoke with
what Ryder thought was an Eastern European
accent. 'My boyfriend is missing.'

'What do you mean, missing?'

This woman was in her early twenties and
he assumed the boyfriend would be a similar age. People that age didn't go missing on
Bondi.

'He went for a swim. I fell asleep. He has
not come back.'

'When was this? How long ago?'

The woman gave a little shrug as if she

wasn't quite sure but her eyes filled with tears, her distress obvious. 'One hour?'

'Where were you sleeping?' Ryder asked.

She pointed to the southern end of the beach and Ryder's heart plummeted. She was pointing towards Backpackers' Rip. 'Can he swim?'

'A little.'

That was not what he wanted to hear.

'What does he look like? Dark hair, blond? Tall, short?' Ryder accompanied his questions with hand gestures. Pointing at her hair, raising his hand high and low but she didn't seem to need his pantomime, her English was accented but good.

'Not as tall as you,' she said as she looked him up and down. 'Smaller. Dark hair.'

'What's his name?'

'Sergei.'

'And what is your name?'

'Mika.'

'Okay, Mika, I want you to take a look and see if you can see him in the water,' Ryder said as he handed her a pair of binoculars. Maybe with some additional magnification she would spot him.

He switched on the radio. 'Ryder to Central. We've got a report of a missing person who might have gone swimming. Possibly in

Backpackers'.' His voice remained calm even though his gut was churning. Had he missed something? He knew Jet would be thinking the same as him.

He turned to Mika, who was standing next to Bluey, binoculars raised. 'Can you see him?'

She shook her head.

'Central, Bluey and I will head out but we need someone to check the beach, the fore-shore, everywhere.' There was a possibility that Sergei wasn't in the water. It was a slim chance but there nonetheless. 'And can you send someone down here with the defib?'

'Copy that,' Jet replied. 'I'll send Dutchy down and get Gibbo to launch the jet-ski.'

There were eight lifeguards on duty and this search and rescue would stretch them thin on other parts of the beach but that was unavoidable. They needed all the manpower they could muster. Ryder knew Jet would call the police as well as the paramedics.

He grabbed one rescue board as Bluey dashed off to pick up one that was stored further along the beach. He ran into the water, threw the board down and leapt on. The swell had dropped, the tide had eased and the water was clear. It was getting late but there was still enough light to ensure good visibility. The lifeguards would have been thinking about packing up soon but that would change now, depending on the outcome of their search.

He looked over his shoulder as he paddled out. He could see Dutchy in one of the buggies, heading for Mika, and he could hear the whine of the jet-ski as Gibbo hit the water.

'Central.' He spoke out loudly, knowing the radio microphone in his armband would relay his words to the tower. 'Tell Gibbo to head out the back, he can check the rip.'

Backpackers' Rip could have carried an unsuspecting swimmer out to sea or Sergei could be stranded on the rocks past Icebergs. Ryder thought that second scenario was unlikely as someone would have alerted the tower, but if he'd been carried out to sea they might never find him.

He kept paddling as he searched the water, top and bottom, but he couldn't quieten the voice in his head, the one that told him that if the swimmer he'd thought he'd seen earlier had been Sergei then there was a good chance that it was going to be too late to save him now.

'What's going on, man?' He looked up to see one of the surfers he'd spoken to earlier paddling towards him.

'We've had a report of a missing person. It's possible he may have gone swimming.'

'Is it the guy you were looking for earlier?'

'Could be. Have any of you helped someone out today? Taken them out of the water?'

'Not me, man, but I'll check with the others. Who are we looking for?'

'A man, slight build, mid-twenties, dark hair.' It was important to know Ryder wasn't looking for a female, or a teenager, or an elderly swimmer, but Ryder knew, in reality, they were looking for a body. A poor swimmer wasn't going to last in the ocean in these conditions for an hour or more, and even a competent swimmer would have become fatigued. If Sergei was in the water they were looking at a recovery exercise and that knowledge weighed heavily on Ryder's conscience.

The surfer nodded and paddled off.

'Gibbo has got nothing.' Jet's voice came through the radio in Ryder's armband.

'We've got nothing either,' Ryder responded. Everyone seemed to be accounted for. Maybe Sergei hadn't gone swimming after all. 'Have you checked the toilet block and showers?'

'Yes, we're covering all bases,' Jet replied, and Ryder could hear what was unsaid. Sergei hadn't been found on dry land and, therefore, he must be in the water. His stomach sat like a stone in his belly.

'I've called Lifesaver One, they're on the way,' Jet added.

Ryder heard the chopper approaching as the surfer returned.

'Most of the guys have only been in the water for about an hour,' the surfer told him, 'and there've been plenty of swimmers with dark hair.' Ryder knew that was always the case, it was like trying to pick a needle out of a haystack if that was his only defining feature. 'But no one has seen anyone in trouble or given anyone any assistance.'

The surfer's information sounded like good news but Ryder's antennae were twitching. He knew how quickly and silently people could drown. If Sergei had been swimming alone, which seemed like the case, he could easily have drowned without anyone noticing.

He thanked the surfer as Lifesaver One appeared over the headland. The helicopter hovered over the ocean, staying high enough above the waves so the wash from its rotors didn't disturb the water.

Ryder and Bluey waited as the chopper

moved slowly overhead but there was nothing to indicate they'd spotted anything untoward.

'Do we keep looking?' Bluey asked.

Ryder nodded. He could see two ambulances and a quick response vehicle parked near the lifeguard tower plus several police cars. Police could be seen combing the beach but there was still no sign of Sergei. Ryder wouldn't give up until it got too dark to see. Or until Sergei was found.

He paddled towards Icebergs Surf Club and drifted over a bed of seaweed near the rocks. The rocks cast shadows on the water and the dark seaweed took on a slightly sinister appearance. Patches of pale sand broke through the blackness, providing some relief. His eyes skimmed the sea bed, looking without really seeing, but as he lifted his head to see if anyone else had had any success something caught his eye. Unsure if it was an irregular shape or an unexpected movement, he looked beneath the surface again.

He peered into the water.

Something pale was moving in the depths. It might have been weed or a stingray or a fish but as his eyes adjusted to the gloom he was filled with dread. Briefly he hoped his eyes were deceiving him but in reality he knew they were not.

He wasn't looking at a patch of sand. Or a fish.

It was a hand. And it was several feet under the surface.

CHAPTER EIGHT

'BLUE! OVER HERE,' he yelled over his shoulder as he slid off his board and dived down to the ocean floor.

The hand belonged to a dark-haired man. Ryder pulled on his arm but the man didn't move. His lungs were burning as he dived deeper. The man's eyes were open, staring lifelessly into the ocean.

He pulled on the man's shorts. This time he moved slightly but he still didn't come free. Ryder looked down. The man's foot was tangled in the seaweed. He was trapped, tethered to the ocean floor. He must have gone under and become stuck.

Ryder surfaced and breathed in deeply, preparing to dive again.

'Have you found him?' Bluey asked.

He nodded. He was certain it was Sergei. It *had* to be Sergei.

'I'll let everyone know.' Bluey's usual

happy disposition was subdued by Ryder's expression. There was no need for further discussion, it was obvious the outcome was a tragic one.

Ryder submerged himself again, this time diving deeper to free Sergei's foot. The weed was thick and slippery and he had to work hard to free it. Sergei must have panicked when the weed had wrapped around his foot. Of course he would have panicked but somehow he had made the situation worse by thrashing about.

He pulled the weed from around Sergei's ankle and then grabbed him under the armpits and dragged him to the surface. He might be slight but he was a dead weight and Ryder's muscles and lungs were screaming by the time he broke through the waves.

Sergei was limp and unresponsive.

Bluey had called for the jet-ski and Ryder and Bluey wrangled the body onto the rescue sled that was towed behind the ski. Gibbo would get him back to shore as quickly as possible so resuscitation could be attempted. They could only assume how long he'd been submerged for and all efforts would have to be made to revive him.

Ryder and Bluey paddled into shore. Ryder was exhausted, mentally and physically drained, but he had to keep going. He hopped off his rescue board in the shallow water and dragged it back to the lifeguard buggy.

Gibbo had brought the jet-ski in nearby and Ryder could see dozens of first responders circling around. There were several paramedics in attendance, Poppy amongst them, as well as an intensive care doctor.

Poppy's blonde hair shone in the afternoon light and guided him up from the water like a beacon. Despite the fact that she had cancelled their plans, despite the fact that she had made it clear that he wasn't her priority, he couldn't prevent his heart rate from escalating when he saw her. He still wanted her, she still stirred him. He hadn't stopped loving her and he knew he wouldn't for a long time. It was possible he would always love her.

She was sitting with Mika, with one arm wrapped around the girl's shoulder. Poppy saw him coming up the beach and she smiled at him but her smile didn't reach her eyes. The afternoon had taken a toll on all of them, most of all Sergei and Mika.

It was getting late and Ryder could feel a slight chill in the air. Normally by this time the crowds on the beach would be starting to thin out but there was still a large number of people hanging around. They were attracted to the drama, wanting to know how the story ended.

In an attempt to give Sergei some privacy the police had erected a screen around him and the mass of first responders. Ryder couldn't get close but he didn't need to. He could hear the resuscitation efforts and while he understood the need for the medics to try their best, he knew, in his gut, it had been too long. Sergei's skin was grey and waxy. It would take a miracle to bring him back.

Ryder's knees were like jelly. Goosebumps covered his skin and he knew he should get warm but his legs weren't steady enough to support him. He knelt in the sand to give himself a minute to recover.

'How are you doing?'

He looked up to find Jet standing in front of him. He was holding out a beach towel and Ryder took it and wrapped it around himself as he tried to stop the shivering.

'I'm okay,' he said, even though he wasn't. He was far from okay, but he wasn't about to have that conversation here, now, on the sand in the midst of the crowd. He didn't want strangers hearing his thoughts. Hearing him confess his regrets. His guilt.

He felt responsible for the situation they found themselves in. Had it been Sergei he'd seen earlier? Had he raised a hand? Had he requested assistance? Had he been to blame? Was there more he could have done?

'You should go up to the tower and get warm,' Jet said.

'In a minute.' Like the rest of the crowd he couldn't make himself move away but he had more invested in the outcome. Not that he thought, for one minute, it would be anything but tragic, but he was going to force himself to stay until the end. He owed Sergei that much.

He got to his feet. There was nothing he could do for Sergei but perhaps there was something he could do for Mika.

He walked over to where Poppy and Mika were sitting and sat beside Poppy. She had Mika wrapped in a space blanket, trying to combat the cold and the shock. An oxygen cylinder stood at the ready. Just in case. He could tell Poppy wanted to shield Mika from the drama, wanted to protect her, but Mika was only half turned away and Ryder could understand her compulsion to watch. As if she could ward off the inevitable if she was brave enough to watch.

Mika looked across at Ryder. 'He is not going to be okay, is he?'

Her voice was flat. She wasn't asking a question but stating a fact.

'I'm sorry,' he said. 'No one saw him go under.'

Ryder sounded exhausted and Poppy knew he was trying to keep his emotions under control. She knew he would be struggling to make sense of the tragedy, knew his mind would be churning with questions, wondering if there was anything else he could have done.

She had seen him pull Sergei to the surface and she could imagine how he was feeling. She had seen plenty of dead bodies in her line of work and she knew Ryder would have seen his fair share too but you never became immune to the suffering, the loss, the effect that someone's passing had on family and loved ones. And with someone who was young, whose death had in all likelihood been avoidable, it was especially difficult to accept.

She could feel the tension in his shoulders, could see it in the set of his jaw, and knew he was fighting to hold himself together. She knew he wouldn't want to lose his composure in public.

She wished she could take him in her arms and make everything better, but for now all she could do was let him know she was there

for him. She slid her free hand under the towel
that was wrapped around his shoulders. Her
fingers found his and she squeezed his hand
gently, reassuring him, trying to comfort him
with her presence, but there was no response
from Ryder. His hand was cold and still. He
didn't react, she got nothing back.

Was he upset with her?

She knew she'd ruined his plans but there
would be other weekends. She'd thought he
would understand. He always had. He always
knew what she was thinking, how she was
feeling, without her having to spell it out for
him.

Perhaps it was just the stress of the day.
Perhaps he wasn't upset with her but upset
with the situation. That was understandable.
She would make it up to him, she promised
herself. This time she would be a shoulder
for him to lean on.

To their credit the medics tried everything
possible in difficult conditions but their resuscitation efforts were in vain. The defibrillator reported no shockable rhythm and the
drugs didn't work. The intensive care special-
ist eventually called time of death and Sergei
was covered with a sheet.

'I need to get Mika to the ambulance,'

Poppy said to Ryder as the other paramedics, lifeguards and police moved Sergei to a stretcher and lifted it, preparing to carry him off the beach. 'I'll meet you at the tower.'

She was loath to leave him but she had a job to do. But the sooner she had Mika sorted the sooner she would be able to give Ryder her attention.

'Come with me, Mika.' She kept her arm wrapped around the woman's shoulders and led her across the sand. She doubted she would be able to walk across the beach without assistance. Without someone to gently encourage her to put one foot in front of the other.

News crews and beachgoers lined the promenade. They were being held back by the police but Poppy also wanted to shield Mika from curious spectators. She had enough to deal with. The emergency services workers were met with silence but Poppy could still feel hundreds of eyes watching them. It was an uncomfortable sensation. As quickly as she could she got Mika sorted, handing her over to a policewoman who would take care of her. Mika didn't need medical attention, the police would look after her, leaving Poppy and her colleague, Alex, free to check on the lifeguards. She passed Mika and Sergei's belongings over and went to tell Alex to meet her in the tower.

Ryder was sitting by the desk, leaning forward, his elbows on his knees, his head in his hands, staring at the floor. Poppy went to him without hesitation. She put her hand on his shoulder and he lifted his head. He looked wiped out, mentally and emotionally exhausted. She stepped closer, between his knees, and held his head against her. She didn't speak. What could she say?

She rubbed his back, her hand making small, firm circles, reassuring him through touch, but Ryder still didn't respond. He had dropped his hands but otherwise was motionless. It was almost as though he was completely unaware of her presence.

Jet had boiled the kettle and handed Ryder and Bluey each a mug of hot coffee. Poppy could smell something else. Whisky? Had he added a dash? It wouldn't hurt.

'What now?' she asked him.

'It's almost seven. Dutchy can close the beach and we'll have a debrief.'

'Ryder and Bluey need to get warm. They need to shower and change.'

Jet nodded. 'They can head to the shower block now, we'll manage the beach.'

Ryder still hadn't spoken and Poppy was

worried. She bent down and kissed him gently, focussing his attention on her for a moment. 'I'll come back after my shift,' she said, 'and take you home with me.'

She would be his sounding board, she would give him someone to lean on, to talk to. It was her turn to listen and this time she would be there for him.

By the time Poppy returned to the lifeguard tower Ryder was showered and dressed. He had changed into jeans and a T-shirt and had thrown a thick, warm jacket over his top but he still felt cold and, if he was honest, he didn't really feel like company. In fact, he'd had deliberated long and hard about whether or not he'd wait for Poppy to come back.

His mind had been spinning in the shower and he'd had trouble sorting through one thought before another one would take over. Could he have done more? Could he have saved Sergei? Life was short, and today's tragedy reinforced that fact. What did he want from his life? What did Poppy want? Did she want him? Did they have a future? Where would they go from here?

He was still trying to process his thoughts when Poppy walked in. If he'd wanted to escape he'd missed his opportunity.

'How's Mika doing?' he asked, forcing himself to say something.

'She's in good hands. She's with a social worker. She'll organise embassy assistance and a translator and whatever else Mika needs.'

Ryder nodded but couldn't find the energy to continue the conversation.

Poppy reached for his hands and tugged him out of the chair. 'Come on, time to go.'

He let her lead him outside. It was easier to stay silent and go with her than to explain how he was feeling. There were things they needed to sort out. Sergei's death had cryst-allised his thoughts in one respect. Life was tenuous and he wasn't prepared to sit around and wait for Poppy to decide if she wanted a relationship with him or not.

He needed to know how she felt.

He loved her and he needed to hear how she felt. He needed to know if she was going to take a chance on love. On him.

He didn't want to lose Poppy but if they didn't have a future he wanted to know.

Ryder hadn't said one word during the drive home and even though it was only a short distance Poppy's concern escalated. He was usually the first to make conversation but his responses to her attempts to talk were monosyllabic at best and once they were inside things didn't improve.

'Are you hungry?' she asked.

'No.'

'I think you should eat something. I'll make cheesy treats. Comfort food.'

He gave her a half-smile in reply but nothing more.

She fed him, hoping food would improve his state of mind. She waited until he had demolished the sandwiches before testing the waters again.

'Any better?'

'Not really.'

She nestled into his side and put her hand on his chest, connecting them together. 'It was a tragic accident,' she said, trying to reassure him. 'Everyone did their best.'

'Did I?' he sighed. 'Do you know I thought I'd seen a raised hand in Backpackers' earlier in the afternoon. I went out looking but didn't find anything. What if that was Sergei? What if I missed something?'

'Why would you think that? Sergei wasn't reported missing until late in the day and no one else saw anything. I was on the beach, listening, when you were searching. No one suspected anything untoward.'

'You know how silently and quickly people drown. What if I could have done more? What if this is my fault? There hasn't been a death from drowning at Bondi for several years.'

'But there have been deaths from other causes. As lifeguards, do you blame yourselves every time?'

'To a degree. Don't you?'

'As a paramedic I've learned that people die. Sometimes we are able to help, sometimes we aren't, but it's not helpful to dwell on the fatalities. We hope to learn from any mistakes but sometimes there is nothing that can be done. Doing our best is all that's possible.'

'I'm not sure that I did my best.'

'Bondi Beach isn't only your responsibility. No one else noticed Sergei in trouble. Not another lifeguard, not the tower, not a surfer. His girlfriend didn't even know. You can't blame yourself.'

'I'm sure Mika does.'

'Oh, Ryder. I don't think anyone will think this is your fault.' She hugged him tightly, wishing she could take his pain away or at least share it. She hated to see him hurting.

'I might not be totally to blame but I have to take some of the responsibility. One minute

Mika and Sergei are enjoying a trip to Australia, a day at the beach, and the next Mika is dealing with her boyfriend's body. It made me think about my life. My mortality. My future. It made me think about what I want. Each of us has limited time and I want to make the most of my life. I want to be happy. I want to make a difference. I want to be someone's priority. I want to be *your* priority.'

Poppy went cold. Her hands trembled and her heart pounded and she knew it was fear.

She needed Ryder, she loved him, but she heard his unspoken words and she couldn't disagree. She hadn't put him first.

She had never told him how she felt. She hadn't told him or shown him. She'd just expected him to know—he'd always known what she was thinking. She'd thought he'd know how she felt, how important he was to her. 'You…'

'I what?' he prompted. 'I am your priority?' He shook his head. 'I don't think so. Your house, your career, your bank balance, you've chosen all of that over me. I shouldn't have been at work today. I was only there because you changed our plans. You chose to go to work instead of spending time with me. If I hadn't been at work maybe Sergei would have been someone else's responsibility. Maybe someone else would have saved him.'

'You're blaming me?'

'No.' He shook his head. 'Not for Sergei. That's my cross to bear. But I don't think you and I want the same things and it makes me wonder what I'm doing here. My job here is temporary and today I didn't even do it well. I've got a job waiting for me in Perth. You've got your house in Brisbane, your career. If we want different things then there's nothing to keep me here.'

'What are you saying?' Poppy was shaking now.

'You need to work out what you want. You need to decide if you have room for me in your life. I had to leave you twelve years ago and I don't want to leave you again but life is short. I don't want to always be waiting.'

'You're leaving?'

'I have a job waiting for me in Perth. It's time.'

'You're going back to Perth!?' He couldn't mean it. He couldn't be talking about leaving her again.

'I've been thinking about my options for a while, today's events just helped to clarify my future for me.'

'No.' She couldn't let him go. She couldn't

lose him. Not again. She needed more time. 'You need to rest. Things won't seem so grim in the morning, they never do.'

'I don't see what will change. In the morning Sergei will still be dead and I'll still be waiting for you to choose me.'

She wasn't ready to let him go. 'Come to bed. Let me comfort you,' she said, but Ryder shook his head.

'No. I'm not going to be good company, I need to be alone.'

She stood in the passage and watched as he walked out the door. The words she knew she should have said stuck in her throat, threatening to choke her. She had lied to herself. Told herself that she didn't want anything serious, that she wouldn't fall in love, but the truth was she'd already been in love. She had always loved Ryder.

Why couldn't she tell him?

She sank to the floor as the door closed behind him. Her legs couldn't support her any longer.

Had that just happened? Had Ryder left her? Had she lost him again?

Tears ran down her face as she grappled with the thought that once more she'd been rejected. But she couldn't blame Ryder. This was all her fault.

He was right. She'd put her house before him. How stupid was she? What was the point of having a home if she didn't have Ryder?

She'd wanted a life that was safe and predictable but that wasn't realistic. Life wasn't safe and predictable and a life without Ryder would mean nothing. She couldn't let him go. She'd give up everything she had if she got to keep Ryder.

She had to let him know.

She thought about going after him but her legs wouldn't move and she knew she needed to work through this. She would only get one chance, she needed to make it count.

She needed a plan. She needed to prepare.

Tomorrow she would put the wheels in motion. She would show Ryder how she felt. She would speak to Craig and agree to put the house on the market, that would be the first step, and then she'd speak to Ryder. She had time. He wouldn't leave her tomorrow.

Ryder sat in the wooden lifeguard tower at Tamarama Beach and tried to concentrate on the ocean. It was a glorious day but even the early morning surf he'd had and the sight of the sun on the ocean couldn't lift his spirits. He was struggling to reconcile himself with Sergei's death and the part he'd had to play.

A lot had gone wrong and he accepted that most of it was not his responsibility. Sergei shouldn't have been swimming at the southern end of the beach but if Mika hadn't fallen asleep it could have been different. If Sergei had been a stronger swimmer, if his foot hadn't got stuck, if someone else had seen something, the outcome could have been very different.

In hindsight he knew he'd done his best and he knew he couldn't change what had happened but next time he'd trust his instincts. But Sergei's death wasn't the only problem. He was in a bad mood and he knew it was because of his uncertainty over Poppy.

Sergei's death had reinforced for him that losing someone you loved had to be the worst pain imaginable and he was terrified he was going to lose Poppy. He'd given her a chance to tell him how she felt and she'd told him nothing.

He'd thought he understood her, sometimes he'd thought he knew her better than she knew herself, but in this case he was flying blind. He'd thought she loved him but he wondered now if he really knew her at all. He had no idea what she was thinking and he could go crazy trying to figure her out.

He didn't want to be without her but a relationship had to be a reciprocal agreement. If she didn't love him then he'd have to accept they were done. They had no future.

If she didn't want him, if she didn't need him, he'd go home. Back to Perth. He wasn't sure that his mother or sister needed him any more either but they were family. He didn't want to leave Poppy, but if she didn't want him he had no reason to stay in Bondi.

He loved her but he'd got over her once before.

He didn't want to do it again but the situation was out of his hands. It was up to Poppy.

He sighed and picked up the binoculars and scanned the surf. Jet had suggested that he take the day off but he'd insisted on keeping his shift. It was better to be busy. It gave him less time to think about Sergei. Less time to think about Poppy.

Tamarama had two permanent rips and was one of Sydney's most treacherous beaches. It was adjacent Bondi, one beach further south, and was staffed by the Bondi lifeguards during the busy summer period. Ryder could see many experienced surfers in the water but it was the inexperienced ones he was keeping under surveillance. He wished there was a way of discouraging novice surfers to avoid

Tamarama but it was a popular surf spot with good consistent waves.

He had his eye trained on a lone surfer who appeared to be drifting south towards Bronte and the notorious rock formation called The Twins. Many surfers had come unstuck in that stretch of ocean. The two tall rocks, The Twins, were separated by a narrow channel of water and the tide created a vortex that, once it took hold of you, sucked you in between the rocks against your will. It was a skill to be able to escape the power of the ocean. Time the waves incorrectly and you'd find yourself thrown against the rocks, putting you at risk of abrasions, broken bones or worse.

He kept his binoculars focussed on the surfer, knowing he needed to paddle north, away from the rocks, back towards the beach. But unless he was a strong swimmer and also aware of the dangers, Ryder knew it would be difficult for him to make it.

Every second that passed saw him pulled closer and closer to the rocks. He saw him begin to paddle and he willed him on but his efforts were in vain. The rip was dragging him further from safety. Closer to danger.

Ryder knew he couldn't wait any longer. The surfer was in trouble.

He stood up and dropped the binoculars on the bench.

'Gibbo, call Central and tell them to send the jet-ski. There's a surfer headed for The Twins.'

He grabbed the rescue tube and flew down the stairs, leaving Gibbo in the tower, knowing that the outcome of this emergency was all up to him. If the surfer was sucked between the two massive rocks there was only one way he was coming out and that would be with Ryder and the rescue tube. The long rescue boards were useless in the narrow gap between the rocks, as were the jet-skis.

The jet-ski would take several minutes to arrive. It needed to travel one and a half kilometres from Bondi to Tamarama and Ryder had no idea if it had been launched today. If it was still on the trailer by the tower, that would add even more precious minutes before it could be of assistance. In any case, in this situation the jet-ski was only useful for transporting a patient back to shore. It was impossible to get near The Twins using the ski. The vortex created by the tide would simply suck the jet-ski in as well, smashing it against the rocks.

Ryder slung the strap of the rescue tube diagonally over his chest and one shoulder, tucked the bright yellow tube under his arm and sprinted down the beach. He ran through the shallow water, threw the tube behind him and dived under the first wave break, surfacing and swimming strongly towards The Twins as the tube floated in his wake, pulled along by the rope.

He swam parallel to the beach, lifting his head every now and then to check his direction. He could see the surfer. He was still trying to paddle away from the rocks but he was making absolutely no progress. He had seconds before he would be sucked in between the rocks.

Ryder swam harder, knowing it was futile. There was no way he could reach him in time.

The next wave was his undoing. It picked the surfer up and swept him into the gap and Ryder lost sight of him.

'Bondi Fifteen, can you head to Tamarama Beach. Lifeguards have requested standby assistance for a water rescue.'

'Copy that,' Poppy said, as she swung the ambulance around and headed towards Tamarama. She parked on the road overlooking the beach. There was a crowd of people standing on the path that ran along the clifftop and stretched from Coogee Beach past Bronte and Tamarama to Bondi and was popular with joggers and walkers. The spectators were all looking to the right, at the southern end of the beach.

She and Alex climbed out of the ambulance and joined the spectators at the clifftop fence. People were pointing at a surfer who was paddling furiously but, despite his efforts, was getting dragged closer and closer to the rocks at the base of the cliff. A lifeguard was closing in on him, cutting through the water with strong strokes, a yellow rescue tube dragging along behind him. The swell was large today, good for surfing but not so good for rescues.

A flash of red in the water to her left caught her eye. She turned her head and could see the Bondi lifeguard jet-ski racing south. She recognised Jet on the back of the jet-ski, his blond curls streaming behind him in the wind. She turned back towards the rocks. She saw the lifeguard pause and lift his head to check on the surfer's location. Her stomach dropped. It looked like Ryder.

She strained her eyes but the distance and the breaking waves made it impossible to see for certain. He had broad shoulders, thick hair that could be either dark blonde or brown. She felt in her gut that it was Ryder, the tilt of his head, the shape of his jaw was familiar, but he shouldn't be working. After the drama of yesterday, after Sergei's drowning, surely Ryder should have been given the day off? What was he doing at work?

'Can I borrow the binos?' she asked. Alex passed the binoculars over and she lifted them to her face.

Her stomach lurched.

It *was* Ryder.

She lowered the binoculars, widening her field of vision. The tide was strong and the surfer was getting pulled further and further away from Ryder.

He was close to the rocks now.

In the blink of an eye he was sucked behind a large rock. Swept out of sight.

Her heart was in her mouth as she saw Ryder put his head down and swim towards the rocks. He followed the surfer, swimming directly into the path of danger until he too disappeared from view.

She held her breath, waiting, willing him to reappear.

It seemed to take for ever, but eventually she saw him, swimming strongly away from the massive rock formation. It was slow going as he dragged the surfer behind him. The yellow rescue tube was around the surfer's chest and the rope attached to the harness stretched tightly from Ryder's shoulders to the tube.

The surfboard was nowhere to be seen as he swam towards the open water.

The jet-ski was stationary in the water. Jet was on the back, sitting behind another life-guard, possibly Dutchy. Why weren't they moving?

She realised they couldn't risk going closer or they'd be putting themselves at risk of getting smashed on the rocks. Ryder was going to have to swim to them.

Poppy checked his progress. The surfer was conscious, floating on his back with one arm held across his chest. He was attempting a half-backstroke movement, trying to swim, but it was clear Ryder was doing the majority of the work. He towed the surfer away from the shore but it was slow going.

She heard the thump-thump-thump of a helicopter and looked up. Lifesaver One appeared, hovering above the ocean. Beneath the chopper the jet-ski was moving again. It had turned ninety degrees and was heading out to sea. Poppy frowned. Where were they going?

And then she saw it. A rogue wave was bearing down on them and the jet-ski was sitting in the impact zone.

Dutchy rode the jet-ski up the face of the

wave, dropping down the other side, the rescue mat flying in his wake.

Poppy eyes followed the path of the wave.

It was heading straight for Ryder and he had absolutely nowhere to go.

Her heart skittered in her chest as she watched in horror as the wave picked him up, lifted him over the surfer and hurled him towards the rocks.

She heard someone scream as Ryder was slammed, head first, into the rock and then sucked into the chasm.

Alex grabbed her arm, squeezing her forearm tight, and she realised she was the one screaming.

The wave collected the surfer next and he disappeared too, into the seething mass of white water at the base of the rocks. Roped together, they were powerless, insignificant against the force of the massive wall of water.

Poppy gripped the fence that ran along the cliff edge, her knuckles white with tension, as she waited, helplessly, for the water to release them. After what seemed like a lifetime one of the men was spat out from its hold.

It was the surfer who reappeared first, easily identified by the yellow tube that was still strapped around his chest.

She waited for Ryder, knowing he'd be

close as he'd still be attached via the rope.
As long as it had held.

She was afraid to breathe, afraid to blink,
afraid to look away. The wind blew off the
ocean and her eyes were stinging but she
didn't turn her head, didn't close her eyes.

The surfer bobbed in the water. He wasn't
trying to swim but this time the current
pulled him away from the shore and eventually Ryder came into view.

He floated in the water.

He wasn't moving.

Waves crashed over his face and still he
was immobile. Surely it was only a matter
of time before he started to sink?

Poppy's heart was racing in her chest, making her feel faint. She bent double as a wave
of nausea overwhelmed her. Bile rose in her
throat as she fought fear.

She wanted to yell out, to tell the surfer to
look out for Ryder, but she couldn't breathe
and she couldn't scream and she knew the
surfer wouldn't be able to hear her anyway.
She was helpless, completely helpless.

She could see the surfer looking around.
Could he feel Ryder's weight dragging on the
rope? She saw when he registered the situation. He pulled on the rope with one hand,
pulling himself towards Ryder and grabbed

him with his good arm and somehow managed to hold his head out of the water.

The jet-ski was coming back for them and Poppy willed them to hurry.

Jet dived off the back off the ski and swam strongly towards Ryder. Poppy raised the binoculars in time to see him hook his arm under Ryder, unclip the rope from the rescue tube and separate the two men. He threw the rope to Dutchy, who pulled it through the water, dragging the surfer to the jet-ski.

Jet was treading water and supporting Ryder. He was limp in the water, lifeless.

Tears streamed down Poppy's cheeks as she silently begged Jet to save him. But what could he do? The jet-ski couldn't manage all of them in these conditions. Not with Ryder unconscious. Or worse.

CHAPTER NINE

JET WAS LOOKING up at the helicopter. He stretched one arm above his head and waved his hand in a circular motion, indicating to the crew that he needed help.

Poppy saw one of the rescue crew drop from the chopper. He landed in the water, feet first, and swam over to Jet. She watched as he and Jet slipped a harness over Ryder. They attached cables and winched Ryder and the rescue operator up to Lifesaver One. Ryder hung limply in the harness, giving Poppy no clue as to his condition.

As the helicopter banked and headed inland, she thought she might be sick. She had never felt so afraid or so helpless in all her life.

This was all her fault.

'Poppy, we need to go.'

Alex prompted her and she turned her attention back to the beach as the chopper flew out of sight. All she could do now was pray that Ryder was okay. She still felt physically sick but she had a job to do.

Dutchy had the jet-ski idling past the breaking waves. Somehow he'd managed to get the surfer onto the rescue mat at the back of the ski and was now waiting for Jet, who was swimming towards him. They'd be bringing the patient into the beach and she and Alex had work to do.

She took a deep breath and tried to steady her nerves as she and Alex grabbed kitbags and a stretcher from the ambulance and headed down to the sand.

The surfer was able to get himself off the rescue mat and walk up the beach but Poppy and Alex went to him, ready to support him if necessary. Over the man's shoulder Poppy mouthed a silent question to Jet. *Ryder?*

She knew, even if her family wasn't as used to lipreading as they were, that Jet would understand her question. He put the tips of his thumb and forefinger together to make a circle, extending his three other fingers.

Okay.

He continued to sign, relaying a silent message. *Took a knock to the head, unconscious but breathing.*

He was alive.

Poppy breathed out and the tightness in her chest dissipated ever so slightly. Injured, but alive. How badly injured, she didn't know, but alive was better than the alternative. So much better.

She turned her attention to the patient. He had several nasty abrasions and was in significant pain with a dislocated shoulder, but after administering pain relief they were able to stabilise him and get him from the beach to the ambulance.

As Poppy pulled the ambulance to a stop in the emergency bay at Bondi General she could see Lily waiting with the team. She opened the rear doors and, while Alex unloaded the stretcher, she signed to Lily. *Was Ryder brought here?* She didn't want to discuss Ryder in front of another patient but she was desperate for news. Sign language allowed them to have a conversation.

Lily nodded.

Had he regained consciousness?

No. He's been taken off for scans.

Poppy longed to see him but she knew that was impossible. For now. She felt sick, completely helpless and utterly powerless.

Will you let me know if you hear anything? Tell him I'll be back as soon as my shift ends.

There was nothing else she could do.

* * *

Poppy burst into the emergency department of Bondi General. She'd had one update from Lily to let her know that Ryder had been admitted for observation after having his scans and that he was stable but still hadn't regained consciousness.

She was frantic, beside herself with worry, and knew she wouldn't relax until she'd seen him with her own eyes. Her concern was tinged with a heavy dose of guilt too. She couldn't shake the thought that Ryder's injury was all her fault.

She knew it was true. If they'd gone away like Ryder had planned he wouldn't have been in the water. He wouldn't have been at risk.

He wasn't supposed to be at work—not yesterday or today. He was supposed to be away with her for the weekend.

There was no denying *she* had put him in that position. She couldn't believe she'd thought it was more important to take the extra shifts at work than to spend time with him. Now she just had to hope she'd have an opportunity to make amends.

She saw Lily standing at the triage desk, waiting for her. Poppy didn't break stride. 'How is he?'

'He's sedated. The scans showed some swelling of his brain but we won't know the full extent of his injuries until he regains consciousness.'

'Can I see him?' She was desperate. Nothing was more important to her than Ryder. Not her mortgage or her job. She'd been a fool.

Lily nodded and led her to his bedside. His eyes were closed and he looked pale under his tan. Poppy could see bruises and abrasions on the right side of his face. He had oxygen tubing under his nose and a dressing on his right shoulder. He was hooked up to various monitors but was breathing on his own. Poppy automatically checked the monitors, making sure the numbers were reasonable as she pulled the solitary chair away from the wall and positioned it next to the bed.

She sat down and reached for his left hand, wrapping her hands around his. She kissed his fingers and squeezed gently, hoping for a reaction, but there was nothing. He was still and silent.

She stroked the back of his hand as tears ran down her face. 'Ryder, I'm so sorry. This is all my fault.'

What if he didn't regain consciousness?

Why hadn't she gone after him last night? Why hadn't she been able to tell him what he'd wanted to hear? Why hadn't she been able to tell him how she felt?

What if she *never* got the chance?

The machines beeped and lights flashed but Poppy ignored them. She was attuned to the sounds of normal rhythms and could block out anything that wasn't sinister.

She was an idiot. A complete idiot. She could have lost him but she refused to contemplate the fact that he might not recover. As long as he was alive she had time to make it up to him.

She rested her head on the bed and promised she would make amends. He had no idea how important he was to her. She hadn't told him and she certainly hadn't shown him. 'Please, be okay. I need you.'

She closed her eyes and held his hand and imagined that they were lying in bed together. Imagined that he was sleeping peacefully and would wake up and make love to her. She wondered if they would have that chance again.

Poppy was stiff and her back was aching but she was afraid to move. It had been several hours but she was afraid to let go of Ryder's hand in case he could feel her touch. She didn't want him to think she had left him. She didn't intend to leave him again and would stay by his side until he woke up.

She stood up but didn't move away. She kept hold of his hand, keeping their connection, as she kissed his forehead. 'I love you, Ryder. I should have told you that.'

The words flowed easily off her tongue now but she knew she had to find the courage to tell him when he woke up.

'I've always loved you.' She hadn't loved anyone else the same way. No one had ever made her feel like Ryder had but she had convinced herself that those feelings weren't real. She'd been sixteen years old, what did a teenager know about real love? But now she understood. It had been real and she wouldn't feel that way about anyone else. Ryder was the only man for her. She loved him and always had.

'I'm scared, Ryder,' she whispered as she sat down again. 'Scared that you won't love me. Scared that you'll leave me.'

'What did you say?'

For a moment Poppy thought she'd imagined the sound of his voice but when she lifted her head she saw his eyes were open and he was looking at her.

'Oh, my God.' He was awake! 'Are you okay?'

Even as the words popped out of her mouth she realised it was a stupid question but before she could say anything else one of the nurses hustled in, forcing her to move away from Ryder's side. She stepped back reluctantly as the nurse checked Ryder's vital signs and started asking questions.

A second nurse and a doctor arrived and Poppy was asked to wait outside as the room filled with hospital staff.

She stood in the corridor, watching through the window, feeling further and further removed from Ryder. She pressed her hand against the glass and rested her forehead on the window and waited and watched as the medical staff ran through their tests.

She waited, hoping he'd ask for her.

But what if he didn't?

She sat in a chair in the corridor as the minutes passed.

She had finally found her voice but what if she didn't get a chance to use it? What if he didn't want to hear what she had to say?

Time passed and still no one came to call her.

What if they really were over?

* * *

'Do you want to stop and grab dinner some-where before we go home?' Poppy asked Lily as she reversed her car out of the car park.

'I thought you weren't feeling well?'

Poppy had been out of sorts all day. She'd cancelled a shift at work, called in sick, which was something she'd *never* done, because she knew she knew she wouldn't be able to con-centrate. She wasn't ill but she did feel nau-seous. She knew it was nerves, anxiety, and she knew she'd brought it on herself. She was worried she'd really mucked everything up with Ryder and that there was no way back.

She hadn't seen him since she'd left the hospital last night. When she'd *had* to leave. Ryder hadn't asked to see her and then he'd been taken off for more scans while she'd waited. Visiting hours had ended before he'd returned to his room and she'd had to leave. She had no excuse to stay. She wasn't family, she wasn't his next of kin, she was nothing.

And she'd heard nothing from him today. Nothing at all.

The best she could get had been updates from Lily when she had been at work.

Thanks to Lily, Poppy knew Ryder was okay. He had some bruising but he'd been cleared of any serious injuries and the swelling of his brain was reducing.

She had intended on going to the hospital once visiting hours started, only to receive a second phone call from Lily telling her that Ryder had discharged himself.

She'd waited, hoping for a call, but Ryder had disappeared.

After that, she hadn't been able to sit still. She'd gone for a surf and called into the lifeguard tower, pretending to visit Jet but really hoping that Ryder might have gone there, but all the activity had done nothing to ease her anxiety.

She'd been happy to collect Lily when she had called saying her car had a flat battery and she needed a lift home. Even the detour to the supermarket had been a welcome distraction.

'I'm fine,' Poppy said in reply to Lily's question. She was still anxious but she didn't feel like going home to stare at the walls while praying that Ryder would get in touch with her.

'Can we drop the shopping off first?' Lily asked. 'That way I can get changed before dinner.'

Poppy nodded and headed home. She parked the car and checked her phone, hoping Ryder might have messaged her and she'd

missed it, even though she knew that was unlikely as she'd been checking her phone every
few minutes for the entire day.

She saw Lily watching her. 'I'm sure he'll
be in touch, Poppy.'

Poppy wished she felt as confident.

'I'll take the shopping in,' Lily told her.
'Why don't you pour us both a drink while
I get changed and I'll meet you on the deck
and we can work out what to do about dinner.'

Poppy shoved her stubbornly silent phone
in her pocket and locked the car. She followed
Lily into the house and continued through the
kitchen, grabbing two glasses and an open
bottle of wine from the fridge, and stepped
out onto the deck.

The sun had set and fairy lights glowed
around the balcony railing. A nest of candles
glowed on the table and soft music played
through the outdoor speakers. Daisy must be
home, she thought.

She turned to go back inside to grab a third
glass and jumped as she heard a voice in the
semi-darkness.

'Hello, Poppy.'

'Ryder!'

He stood up from his seat in the corner of
the deck.

Why was he here?

'Is everything okay?' she asked.

'Everything is fine.'

'You're okay?'

'I'm fine,' he said as he took two steps towards her, closing the gap while she stood, stunned and surprised and fixed to the spot.

As her eyes adjusted to the gloom she could see the bruises on his face but his blue eyes were clear and bright and if she ignored the cuts and bruises he looked like his old self. His face was bruised but he was still gorgeous and, best of all, he was here and he was smiling.

She studied him closely. She wanted to touch him, she wanted to feel his face, to make sure he was really real and in one piece, but she didn't want to hurt him and she didn't want to overstep any boundaries that she might not be aware of. 'Are you really all right?'

He nodded as he lifted the wine and the glasses from her hand and put them on the table beside the candles. Her heart skipped a beat as his fingers brushed against hers.

'I was so scared,' she said.

'I know.'

'How do you know?'

'I heard you. In the hospital.'

Oh, God, how much had he heard?

'I thought you were asleep.'

'I'm glad I wasn't. I wouldn't know what you were thinking if I hadn't woken up to the sound of your voice.'

'It was easy to talk to you when I thought you were asleep.'

'Do I frighten you that much?'

'No, but the way you make me feel scares me.'

'Why?'

She couldn't speak. She'd been desperate to see him but now the old familiar fear that her love wouldn't be wanted haunted her and made her mute.

'Be brave, Poppy,' he said. 'Tell me how you're feeling.'

But she couldn't do it. Not yet.

'If you're scared, how about I go first?' As always, he knew exactly what thoughts were in her head. She still had no idea how he did that. 'Sit with me and I'll tell you what I'm thinking. How I'm feeling,' he said as he guided her to the seats. 'Do you want me to start off?'

She nodded.

'It hurt to know your house was more important to you than I was. I was upset that you chose to work instead of spending the weekend with me.'

Poppy's heart sank like a stone. That was not what she had hoped or expected to hear. 'Oh, Ryder, I never meant to hurt you.' She was distraught. Mortified. 'I wish I could take it all back.' But she knew she couldn't. It was too late for that. It was done.

'But what hurts the most is that you can't share your feelings with me.'

'I've ruined everything, haven't I?'

He smiled at her. 'I'm not going to give up on you that easily. Not after waiting twelve years. I fell in love with you when I was seventeen. Did you know that?'

'No.' Her heart lightened a little. 'I loved you too.' Past tense was easier. She could do this. 'Do you think how we felt was real?'

'I do. I think how I feel now is real too.'

'How do you know?'

'Take my hand, close your eyes and tell me what you feel.'

He held his hand out to her and she took it. She closed her eyes as he wrapped his fingers around hers and joined them together. 'I can't tell where I finish and you start.' They were one. 'I feel like this is where I belong. With you,' she said as she opened her eyes again.

'This is *exactly* where you belong. You're home. We've come home to each other. Home isn't always a house. It's a place where you are safe and loved. Where the people who matter to you are. Home is a feeling. I understand your need for security and stability but you can get that from things other than a house. There are other ways and there are things that are more important.'

'Like?'

'Like love. You need love, Poppy. You need someone to love you. And that someone is me. *I* love you.'

'You love me?'

'I do. With every last battered and bruised piece of me. And now it's your turn.'

He loved her! The idea made her heart sing with delight. The knowledge made her brave.

'I was scared that you wouldn't love me. That you would think I'm not worthy of love.'

'Why on earth would you think that?'

'My parents never seemed to love us and I never believed you would love me,' she admitted. 'No one seems to need me and I didn't want to need anyone either. I loved you before and you left me and broke my heart. I didn't want to be in love again, I didn't want to be vulnerable.'

'I'm not going to hurt you.'

'But you are going to leave me. You're going back to Perth.'

He shook his head, wincing slightly at

the movement. 'I don't want to go anywhere without you. I've been waiting twelve years to find my way back to you. What happens next is up to you. You said you loved me before. Do you think you could love me again?'

'You were my first love and I've always kept a piece of you, the idea of you in my heart.' She took a deep breath. This was it. The biggest moment in her life. 'I've never stopped loving you. I loved you then and I love you now.'

'That wasn't so hard, was it?'

Ryder was laughing and Poppy laughed with him. 'Not as hard as I thought. It might even get easier with practice.'

He tugged on her hand and pulled her close. 'I'm pleased to hear that and just so you know, I'm not going anywhere. I'm not going to hurt you, or leave you. Not ever. I promise.'

'But what about Perth?'

'There will be other jobs. It doesn't matter to me where I work or where I am as long as you are with me. Nothing matters as long as we're together.' He kissed her as if they'd been apart for months, not hours, and only let her go to say, 'So, where will we go? Here, Perth or Brisbane?'

'Brisbane?'

He nodded. 'If you have your heart set on going back to Brisbane, I could look for a job there instead. I don't want you to have to choose between me and your house again.'

Poppy laughed. 'Don't worry. I've learned my lesson. I've spoken to Craig and told him to put the house on the market.'

'You have?'

She nodded.

'Are you sure?'

'I'm positive. It's done. I had a moment of clarity the other night, watching you walking out my front door. You were right. It's just a house. My home is with you, wherever you are. I know that.'

'So, we have a plan. Our plan. For now we will stay in Sydney and I will be yours. I will be the one who makes you happy. I will be the person you depend on. The one you turn to. The one who makes you smile and laugh. The one who loves you.'

'That sounds perfect.' She was grinning from ear to ear.

'Which leaves just one more thing,' he said as he stood up from the seat and got down on one knee.

'What are you doing!?'

'Something I had planned to do this week-end before you moved the goalposts. This isn't quite how I envisaged this would go but I don't want to wait. I need to prove to you that I am committed, that I am here for you, always, no matter what,' he said. 'Poppy Carlson, I have loved you for as long as I can remember. I have never loved anyone the way I love you and I want our love to last a lifetime. I want to be by your side for eternity. Will you marry me?'

Tears welled in Poppy's eyes but she was smiling as she pulled Ryder to his feet.

'I gave you my heart twelve years ago,' she said, 'and now I give you the rest of me. Everything I am, everything I have, I give to you. I give you my heart, my body and my soul, now and for ever.'

She took a deep breath. She was still scared but she knew she could do this. With his love she could be brave, she could be happy, she could be anything she wanted. She looked into his eyes and said, 'I love you, Ryder, and I always will. We belong together and I don't ever want to be apart again. I never thought I cared about being married but if I get to be married to you then I will gladly spend the rest of my life by your side. You have brought me home and so, my love, my answer is yes. Yes, I will marry you.'

She could hear people clapping as she

kissed him and then they were both enveloped in the arms of her siblings. Daisy was crying, Lily was smiling and Jet was high-fiving Ryder.

'What are you all doing here?' Poppy hadn't realised they'd had an audience. She'd been aware of nothing except Ryder.

'I asked them to come,' Ryder told her. 'I was hoping you'd say yes and I thought you might want to celebrate with your family.'

'You all knew about this?'

All three of them nodded.

'Your car didn't have a flat battery, did it?' she said to Lily, realising her siblings had all had a hand in the evening's events.

Lily shook her head. 'I needed an excuse to get you out of the house to give Ryder time to get here and prepare the surprise.'

Ryde took her hand and said, 'I know you don't like surprises but I thought you'd be okay with this one.'

Poppy smiled through her tears as she gazed at him. 'I'm definitely okay with this one. It couldn't be any better. It's perfect,' she said as she wrapped her arms around him and whispered into his ear, '*You're* perfect and I love you. Now and always.'

* * * * *